"I want a

"Like who is still after me," she continued. "Who tried to run us down, and most importantly, why won't you look at me?"

"They have a video image of the driver from the hospital and are sending it to local police departments for identification," Quinn said. "That should help them narrow down the suspect list."

"And you won't look at me because...?"

"You're imagining things."

"Look me in the eye and say that."

He snapped his attention to her, his blue eyes aflame with anger. "Let's see, the fact I shouldn't have let you leave this room for the SAR mission and I shouldn't have left your side at the hospital because the thought of..." He shook his head.

"What?" She squeezed his upper arm.

"The thought of you being hit by a car because I wasn't there is tearing me apart."

"What would you have done? Would you have stopped the car with your bare hands?"

He gently gripped her shoulders and looked deep into her eyes. "I could have protected you."

Books by Hope White

Love Inspired Suspense

Hidden in Shadows
Witness on the Run
Christmas Haven
Small Town Protector
Safe Harbor
*Mountain Rescue

*Echo Mountain

HOPE WHITE

An eternal optimist, Hope White was born and raised in the Midwest. She began spinning tales of intrigue and adventure when she was in grade school, and wrote her first book when she was eleven—a thriller that ended with a mysterious phone call the reader never heard!

She and her college sweetheart have been married for thirty years and are blessed with two wonderful sons, two feisty cats and a bossy border collie.

When not dreaming up inspirational tales, Hope enjoys hiking, sipping tea with friends and going to the movies. She loves to hear from readers, who can contact her at hopewhiteauthor@gmail.com.

MOUNTAIN RESCUE

HOPE WHITE

HARLEQUIN® LOVE INSPIRED® SUSPENSE

Recycling programs for this product may not exist in your area.

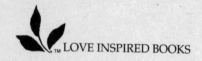

™ LOVE INSPIRED BOOKS

ISBN-13: 978-0-373-44614-8

MOUNTAIN RESCUE

www.Harlequin.com

Printed in U.S.A.

Whoever does not love does not know God,
because God is love.
—*1 John* 4:8

To Dr. James Keen for answering my medical research questions, and SAR volunteer Doug Caley for his insight into this special world.

ONE

Her husband was dead.

Billie Bronson stood on the Cascade Mountain trail overlooking the steep drop down the side of the mountain. She took a deep breath and finally released the pain weighing heavy on her heart.

Pain. Anguish. Dread.

There, she'd finally admitted it. She'd been living under a cloud of dread during the last year of her marriage, nervous about Rick's volatile moods and erratic behavior.

She tugged her fleece hat down to cover her ears. It felt as if the temperature had dropped ten degrees since she'd started out on her hike. But she had to finish this, had to visit the site where Rick had spent his last hours in her arms.

It had taken her a year to get to this place emotionally, the place where she accepted that what she needed most was closure. Closure and forgiveness.

"And I do forgive you," she whispered, hugging herself. Forgiveness was a step toward grace, and it would help her heal.

Still, there were those occasional moments when she'd lie awake at night wondering if she could have done something to stop him from his downward spiral.

She glanced at the plateau below where Rick had shivered and groaned as she'd portioned out food to sustain them both until help had arrived.

If only they hadn't argued; if only he hadn't stormed off

and tripped, falling over the edge and hitting his head on a rock below. But you can't rewind the past, no matter how much you want to.

A sudden flash of Quinn's blue eyes and confident smile haunted her thoughts. No, she wouldn't think about search-and-rescue volunteer Quinn Donovan, not today. He may have rescued her from the mountains and helped her get back on her feet by giving her a place to live, but he was another lost soul like Rick, running from his pain.

"It's good that I left," she whispered.

She'd only seen Quinn sporadically since she'd started her new job at the Echo Mountain Resort. They'd agreed it was the best thing to do, the right thing, because they both had suspected she was leaning on him a little too much after he'd rescued her.

She was falling for him.

But she wouldn't make the mistake of thinking what they had was anything more than an emotional condition brought on by trauma. Billie was smarter than that.

A sudden gust of wind whipped through the mountain pass. If she were so smart, she wouldn't have gone hiking by herself. Although her friend Bree had offered to join her, letting go of the past wasn't something you did with an audience. She interlaced her gloved fingers and closed her eyes. She said a prayer in an effort to completely let go.

"Lord, please help me make peace with Rick's mistakes, with my own failures as a wife and—"

Snap!

She spun around and peered into the mass of trees to her left, but saw nothing, no wild animal or hiker. The hair pricked at the back of her neck.

"Sorry to interrupt," a deep male voice said.

She spotted a man coming up the trail and relief washed over. It was a hiker, probably seeking solitude, like Billie.

"I'll just…" The man motioned that he'd trek past her and give her privacy.

She stepped aside to let him pass. He was tall, about six feet, in his forties with brown hair combed back and a full beard. She noticed his lack of sensible gear. He wore a denim jacket over a purple University of Washington sweat-shirt and sneakers instead of hiking boots. He wasn't even wearing a hat.

Billie assumed he was a tourist passing through town on his way to Vancouver. Travelers often stopped in the town of Echo Mountain for day hikes in the North Cascades.

Yes, he was definitely a tourist. A seasoned hiker would be better prepared with warmer clothing and a backpack.

With a polite smile he edged past her and followed the trail. She thought about suggesting he go back to town, warning him that he was ill prepared for a mountain hike, especially when the weather seemed to be turning cooler, but she didn't want to seem judgmental. He hiked about ten feet and hesitated.

"Hang on," he said and turned to her. "I know you. You're that woman who was stranded out here with her husband."

Billie glanced at the ground, still ashamed that she'd been unable to save Rick's life.

"That was you, wasn't it?" he pressed.

"Yes, it was."

She'd been a local celebrity of sorts for weeks after the rescue. Everyone wanted to know how she'd survived, how she'd managed to keep Rick alive until the search-and-rescue team found them. All that attention made her uncomfortable, which is why she'd welcomed getting out of town and moving into Quinn's coach house.

"That must have been a traumatic experience, watching your husband die like that."

"Actually, he died at the hospital," she said, defending her failed efforts to treat his injuries.

"Oh, sorry."

"Thank you."

"Actually, I knew Rick," he offered.

"You did?" She glanced up.

"Sure, he did some work for me. Seemed like a good guy. I would think you'd be too traumatized to return to this place."

"Yes, well, there's something to be said for closure."

"Oh, I think you came out here for more than closure," he said, his voice taking on a sharp edge.

He stepped closer and goose bumps prickled her arms.

"I think your husband left something behind and you came out here to get it," he said.

"Excuse me?" A shudder racked her body as she edged away from him.

"And it's worth a lot of money," he growled.

Before she could take another step, he grabbed her arm in a viselike grip and shoved her against a tree. She cast a quick glance over her shoulder at the steep drop.

He leaned close. "Don't run. I think we'd make a great team."

His hot, stale breath on her cheek shot panic through her body. With a guttural cry she jammed the heel of her hiking boot against the top of his foot, stunning him enough to loosen his grip. She spun around and took off down the trail.

"Where are you going?" he called after her.

She had better gear, hiking experience and good instincts, but he had brute strength and what she assumed was a motivation to do her harm: retrieving something worth a lot of money. What had her husband gotten himself into?

"I said...where are you going?"

A firm hand clamped down on her shoulder.

"No!" She jerked away and lost her balance.

Arms flailing, she lunged forward, hoping to grab something to keep from careening down the mountainside. Instead, she caught air as she skidded over the edge.

She cried out as she tumbled downward, her pack cushioning her fall. She willed her body to relax knowing that tensing would only increase her injuries.

Injuries? She should be more worried about her attacker, who was probably carrying a weapon in his denim jacket.

She came to an abrupt stop and gasped for air. Tears rolled down her cheeks, not so much from the pain but from the realization she hadn't come close to accomplishing what she'd hoped to in this lifetime. Like her husband, Billie had made her own share of bad decisions.

Like falling for Quinn Donovan.

Unbelievable. She was bruised and battered, possibly going to die so close to where Rick had suffered life-threatening injuries, yet she was thinking about Quinn, his warm eyes that grayed when he was upset, eyes that sparkled bright blue when confident or pleased. Blue, like the sky peeking through the western hemlock and Douglas fir trees towering above.

"Stay conscious," she ordered herself. She had enough presence of mind to reach into her pocket and activate the personal locator beacon that would alert her friend Bree that she was in trouble.

A gray fog drifted through the trees like a curtain, similar to the one drifting across her mind, muddling her thoughts, her prayers.

"Please, God…"

She struggled to focus, to hold on to a sense of time and place. She couldn't pass out, not yet.

In her last moments of consciousness, maybe even the last moments of her life, she struggled to pray, but the prayer was not for herself.

"Help…Quinn," she whispered.

And the world faded to black.

* * *

Quinn had sent Billie away months ago for her own good, yet she lay at the bottom of a mountain trail so very still and motionless…and dead?

No, Quinn would not accept that.

"I'm going down," he said, gripping the rope with both hands.

"Maybe you should wait for the rest of the team," Artie Meyers suggested.

Quinn and Artie were the first to arrive. Not a surprise since it was the middle of the day when most Snoquamish County Search and Rescue volunteers were at work. More would be coming soon, but as one of the first two at the scene, Quinn took the field command position. That's about as far as normal protocol would matter to Quinn today. He wouldn't get bogged down by procedure, not with Billie's life at stake.

"I'll radio when I get to her." Quinn nodded at the middle-age man and started his descent.

Quinn had to pretend this was a routine rescue, that Billie wasn't lying broken and bleeding on the plateau below. He had to act as if the injured party wasn't the woman he'd rescued over a year ago and taken into his life to help her get back on her feet.

The only woman who'd touched a spot inside of Quinn that he thought had been destroyed by a brutal childhood, war and loss.

He shifted his boots against the mountainside and steadied his descent, trying to rein in his panic. He needed to get control of his thoughts, needed to think of Billie as a random, injured hiker.

The text he'd received half an hour ago flashed across his mind: Female victim, thirties, fell while hiking. He hadn't been sure he'd be able to leave his business meeting to join the team.

Then Aiden, Quinn's friend and Billie's boss, sent another text: the victim was Billie.

Billie knew better than to take off into the mountains without hiking buddies. The rule was at least three in a group so that if someone was injured, one hiker could stay with the immobilized party while the third person went for help.

Billie was smart and sensible, yet she'd fallen off a trail close to where she and her husband had been stranded for days, and her husband had sustained a blow to the head from a fall that ultimately took his life.

Was this some kind of penance? Return to the scene where she'd been unable to save her husband in order to drive home her personal failure?

The rope slipped between his gloved fingers and he tightened his grip. He had to focus on helping the victim and stop analyzing his friend's motivations for coming out here alone.

A friend? Is that what she was? The frantic beating of his heart when he'd read Aiden's text indicated otherwise. Quinn couldn't remember driving to the trailhead, or specifics of the conversation he'd had with Aiden. Everything was a blur except the rope between his fingers and the chill seeping through his jacket.

And, of course, the thought of Billie lying on a mountain plateau bruised and broken, and no doubt terrified.

But alive. God, please let her be alive.

Back up, buddy. God doesn't listen to guys like you, remember?

He must have dropped a good fifty feet before he touched down. Corralling his panic at what he'd see when he examined Billie up close, Quinn took a deep breath and kneeled beside her still body.

"Billie?" he said, brushing copper-streaked dark brown hair off her cheek. "Can you hear me, sweetheart?" The endearment slipped out.

He pulled off his glove with his teeth and pressed his fingers against her neck. He realized he held his breath.

A strong and steady pulse beat against his fingertips. A sigh of relief escaped his lips.

"Thank you," he whispered, not sure if he was thanking God for watching over her or thanking Billie for her incredible strength.

He cleared his throat and pressed the button on his radio. "The victim's alive. Send a litter down ASAP, over."

"Roger that. How many team members will you need to secure her to the litter and lift her up, over?"

"It's a small area. I can manage it by myself."

"Roger."

Quinn took off his pack and pulled out a thermal blanket. He covered Billie, tucking the blanket snugly around her body. Glancing at the sky, he hoped the weather would hold until they got her out of here. They'd strap her securely to the litter and raise her to the trail. Her injuries would determine how they'd get her out of here, either by helo or ambulance.

A moan drew his attention to Billie. She opened her normally colorful eyes—usually rich with hues of amber, green and warm brown—now a dull dark gray.

He forced a smile. "We have to stop meeting like this, Wilhelma."

"Quinn? What are you doing here?"

She must be in pain if she wasn't scolding him for calling her by her full name, a name she disliked. "I'm on speed dial for damsels in distress, remember?"

"Yeah, right." She closed her eyes.

He couldn't admit the truth: that after Billie got the job at one of Quinn's properties, Quinn asked his friend and resort manager Aiden McBride to keep Quinn in the loop. In other words, let Quinn know how Billie was doing.

Quinn couldn't help himself. He'd felt a connection to

her, a connection he chose to ignore because he excelled at hurting the people closest to him. He'd already hurt Billie in so many ways, ways she didn't even know about.

Even though Quinn kept his distance from Billie, he'd appreciated the updates from Aiden: Billie excelled at her job as a restaurant hostess, was making friends in the community and was active in the local church. She had blossomed after leaving Quinn's life. He was glad, even if some days he missed her so much it physically hurt.

"Injuries?" he asked her.

"Head mostly. I'm okay." She tried to sit up.

"Lie down. You don't want me to get in trouble for not following protocol."

"Fine." She lowered herself to the ground. "How did you get here so quickly?"

"I was in a business meeting nearby. Aiden texted me after Bree got the alert from your personal locator beacon. She would have been here, but she was stuck up north on business. Sheriff's office also got a call from another hiker who saw you fall."

"Another hiker." She opened her eyes, panicked. "Did he see the guy who attacked me?"

Every muscle in Quinn's body tensed. "Someone attacked you?"

"He grabbed me and I pulled away and lost my footing. He was wearing a denim jacket and gym shoes and he asked me about Rick, and…and…"

Her breathing sped up and her cheeks flushed. Quinn guessed her blood pressure was in the triple digits.

"Shh." He placed an open palm against her cheek. "We'll deal with that later. Right now you've got to lie still and relax."

With a few shallow breaths she closed her eyes and leaned into his touch. The feel of her skin against his hand spread warmth up his arm. No other woman had this kind of effect on him. A part of Quinn ached to explore the dynamic further, but he'd never do that to Billie.

She suddenly turned her head, breaking the connection.

"What's wrong?" he asked.

"Nothing."

"Try again."

She opened her eyes, now tinted with amber and golden hues. He relaxed a little.

"You don't believe me about the man on the trail."

"I do believe you, but I'd like to deal with one thing at a time. I know you're the master multitasker, but I've got a guy's brain, remember?"

He thought she smiled. He hoped she smiled.

"We'll get you to the hospital, then we'll deal with the mystery hiker," Quinn said. Although he hadn't a clue how he was going to control himself if he ever came face-to-face with the guy.

"I'm afraid," she whispered.

"He's not here. It's just me."

Quinn assumed she wasn't afraid of him, yet he wouldn't blame her if she were.

She sighed. "Quinn, if my injuries are worse than they seem and I don't—"

"Stop it," Quinn ordered, because if she didn't make it…

He wouldn't be able to survive that kind of pain.

"But, Quinn," she started, "you should know that the hiker accused me of coming out here to get something Rick left behind."

She obviously couldn't stop thinking about the threat so he encouraged her to continue. "Left something? Like what?"

"I have no idea. Something worth a lot of money apparently."

"Why *did* you come out here?"

"I was hiking."

"Alone?"

"I needed closure."

Quinn leaned back on his heels. Closure was something he'd wished for with so many people in his life, especially his mom, who died when he was a kid.

He glanced at the ridge above, then at Billie. "So, was it worth it?"

"You're making fun of me?"

"No, I'm not, although I was hoping to make you smile."

"This isn't funny. The guy said we'd make a good team. He was creepy and his breath smelled awful and he shoved me against a tree, and I thought, I thought—"

"Shh." He touched her shoulder. "He's gone. No one's going to hurt you while I'm here."

She sighed and looked away. They both knew that wasn't true since Quinn could hurt her worst of all. Not physically, but in every other way that mattered. He couldn't give Billie the sincere love and devotion she deserved. He was incapable of such feelings, incapable of opening his heart to a woman. After everything Billie had been through, she deserved a loving man with integrity.

"I hate this," she muttered.

"The pain?"

"No, I meant I'm sorry to be inconveniencing everyone, making them drop whatever they're doing to come out and rescue me."

"It's not an inconvenience. They live for this stuff—you know that."

"Well, I'm embarrassed that I need their help."

"There's nothing wrong with accepting help, Billie."

She chuckled and clutched her wrist to her chest, pinching her eyes shut.

"What's so funny?" he asked.

"You giving me a pep talk about accepting help from others."

She was right, of course. Quinn was not the type to seek counsel or ask anyone for help. A few seconds passed and he wondered if she'd lost consciousness. He was about to speak her name.

"Thank you," she suddenly whispered.

"For what?"

"For saving me…again."

"I haven't saved you yet," Quinn said, trying to lighten the mood.

She opened her eyes and he could tell she struggled to crack a smile. She was in pain and it was driving him nuts.

He yanked the radio off his belt. "Artie, where's that litter, over?"

"The guys just got here, over."

Quinn turned to Billie. "Saving you is getting to be a full-time job, Ms. Bronson."

"Don't worry, this will be the last time," she said, her tone flat.

"Hey, I was—"

"Kidding, I know." She cracked a sad smile. "But I wasn't."

That sounded awfully final, as if she no longer wanted him helping her, being there for her. "I don't mind playing hero where you're concerned."

"Maybe I do. Maybe I mind depending on you because it makes me feel weak and naive. You won't be there forever, or even tomorrow, or—"

"Hey, calm down."

"I'll be calm when you get me out of here," she snapped.

He wondered if a head injury was causing the edge to her normally affable personality. She suddenly didn't seem like herself.

Not taking his eyes off her, Quinn stood and reached for the radio to see what was taking so long.

"Quinn!" she cried, her eyes rounding with fear.

He glanced up and caught sight of something careening

toward them. There was no way to dodge what looked like a large piece of equipment without leaving Billie exposed, making her the prime target.

"Close your eyes!" He instinctively threw himself over her body like a human shield and clenched his jaw in anticipation of the impending blow.

TWO

Adrenaline rushed through Billie's body and strangled her vocal cords. One minute she was setting her boundaries, letting Quinn know he didn't need to feel obligated to her in any way. The next, she saw something barreling down the side of the mountain—straight at them.

She wasn't sure what she expected Quinn to do, but throwing himself on top of her wouldn't have been her first guess.

"Quinn?" she said.

His warm breath tickled the side of her neck as he exhaled. Was he unconscious?

"Quinn, are you okay?"

He groaned. "What was that?"

"The litter, I think."

"I'm gonna be sore tomorrow."

She realized they'd never been this physically close before. She'd practically lived at his lake house as his personal assistant, but they'd never touched except for a polite hug now and then.

His body, pressed against hers, felt solid and comforting. But she couldn't afford to enjoy it too much.

"Are you hurt?" she asked.

He tipped his head back to look at her. He was so close she could see the gray specs in his blue eyes.

"It nailed me in the back, but I'm okay," he said.

"Then would you mind…?"

"I'm heavy, right. Sorry, I'm probably crushing you."

She didn't correct him. It wasn't his weight that bothered her as much as the ache of wanting something she could never have with this man.

Shifting off her, he stood and clenched his jaw as he pressed his hand against his back. He yanked the radio off his belt with his other hand.

"Artie, what's going on up there?"

No response. Quinn glanced at Billie and she started to sit up again.

"Hey, hey," Quinn said, putting out his hand to stop her.

"The litter's gone and it'll be dark in a few hours. I'm not spending the night here, Quinn. I can't," her voice cracked.

"You won't. I'll get you out of here." He tried the radio again. "Artie?"

A few tense seconds passed. "Sorry, Quinn. A new guy messed up."

"Then they shouldn't have approved him for fieldwork." Quinn sighed, shaking his head. "Have you got another litter, over?"

"Sending one down now, over."

"Roger that." He glanced at Billie. "You're going to be okay."

She closed her eyes and took a deep breath, relieved that she'd be lifted out of here instead of having to climb her way out.

The search-and-rescue team would take her to the hospital where Quinn could absolve himself of his responsibilities. She knew he wasn't here because he cared about her. He was here because Billie had become his pet project ever since he'd rescued her last year. He'd given her a job and a place to live, away from her local notoriety. He'd helped her find solid ground during a turbulent time in her life.

She'd always be grateful to Quinn for that, but she had to make it clear that it was time for both of them to move on. Alone.

Between the doctor's examination, tests and giving her statement to the police about the man on the trail, six hours had passed and she still hadn't had a chance to speak with Quinn alone. She wanted a private moment to set the boundary between them that she needed so desperately to define. Sure, he'd stuck close since the rescue, practically tailgating the ambulance to the hospital. He'd even tried pushing his way into the examining area but security managed to keep him out—at her request.

The sooner she distanced herself the better for both of them. But she wouldn't humiliate him by having that conversation in front of strangers.

It was a necessary conversation. She was done being dependent on men who kept her at an emotional arm's length. When she'd worked for him, Quinn had never missed an opportunity to remind her that he'd never be foolish enough to settle down with one woman.

Then why did he keep showing up to save her? It was a coincidence, that's all. He happened to be nearby and responded to the text alert.

Stop thinking about him and focus on protecting yourself from Rick's questionable business practices.

The man on the trail said Rick had worked for him. Doing what, some type of illegitimate activity? Her attacker accused Billie of going into the mountains to get something Rick had left behind worth a lot of money. But a sensible person wouldn't hide something in the wilderness that could be destroyed by animals or weather.

The first thing she'd do after being released from the hospital would be to dig into Rick's accounts. She'd abandoned her life after the accident because her insides had been so tangled in grief and regret, confusion and shame. Yet maybe a part of her was afraid to find out how far he had fallen.

She couldn't do it any longer, especially since Rick's business seemed to be putting her life at risk. Maybe she should leave Echo Mountain and conduct her investigation from a safe location in a different part of the country.

Which meant finding a new job and making new friends, again. She sighed at the thought. She'd grown close to Bree, her boss's sister and was finally feeling a part of the community and Echo Mountain Church. She didn't want to think about moving again, although it could be the best option to remain safe.

Another option would be hiring a private investigator to dig into her husband's accounts. If only she had the budget to afford one. Knowing what Rick was involved in could help Billie anticipate what was coming next and protect herself.

The things you didn't see coming were the most dangerous of all, things like Rick's sudden personality change and questionable behavior.

And Billie's imprudent attraction to Quinn Donovan.

She'd been so relieved earlier today when she'd regained consciousness and seen Quinn staring down at her with worry in his eyes. She'd almost thought she was dreaming.

She was not only relieved but also surprised. After she'd left Waverly Harbor, she never thought she'd see him again. Oh, he'd texted her a few times to make sure she was okay and had settled comfortably into her new life.

She'd purposely kept her responses to his text messages polite but short and didn't dare ask about his life. She didn't want to know about his latest conquests, either in business or in the romance department.

A doctor in his mid-fifties with a gentle smile stepped into the examining area. "I'm Dr. Green. So, Wilhelma, are you on any medications or have you had any medical issues we should know about?"

"Please, call me Billie. No, no medications. I'm pretty healthy."

"And extremely lucky. You don't seem to have sustained any serious injuries from the fall, but you do have bruised ribs, a sprained wrist and slight concussion."

"Great, then you're releasing me?"

"I'd prefer you stay overnight for observation. Your injuries have the potential for complications."

"I'd rather not. I have to—"

"She'll stay," Quinn said, stepping around the corner into the examining area.

"You're not supposed to be here," she snapped.

The doctor glanced from Quinn to Billie. "Do I need to call security?"

Billie crossed her arms over her chest and stared straight ahead. "No, it's fine."

Quinn extended his hand to the doctor. "Quinn Donovan. I'm with search and rescue. I helped retrieve Billie. Believe it or not, we're friends."

The doctor glanced at Billie for confirmation.

"It's true," she said.

"Fine, well, they'll come to move you to a room shortly," the doctor said.

"Do I really need to stay?"

"We need to keep an eye on swelling of the tissue, both in the lungs and brain, which could lead to more serious problems. Twenty-four hours to be safe." Dr. Green nodded at Billie and left.

Quinn stepped closer to the bed. "What's the rush to get out of here?"

"I don't like hospitals."

"It's more than that. Are you worried the guy from the

trail is going to track you down? Because I won't let that happen. I'm staying with you until you're released."

"That's not necessary," she said a little too sharply. "I'm not worrying about him, but I want to get out and start investigating what he said about Rick."

"Investigating?"

"Yes, I need to figure out what Rick was into and why that man approached me on the trail."

"No, I won't allow it."

"Excuse me?" She half chuckled, wincing at the pain in her chest.

"It's too dangerous."

"It's more dangerous if I do nothing."

He leaned closer. "You don't know what your husband was into. If you go digging into his business you'll risk stirring up all sorts of trouble. You need to hire someone to do that for you, like a retired cop or a P.I."

"I don't have the budget to—"

"I'll take care of it."

"Absolutely not."

"Billie—"

"Not happening, Quinn. I won't let you keep paying for things and taking care of me. I'm not a charity case and I resent being treated like one."

He jerked back as if she'd physically slapped him. She regretted the words, but they had to be said.

"I'm just trying to help," he said.

"You have. You've rescued me twice now. You've done more than enough. So please, go back to Waverly Harbor and leave me to manage my own life."

Quinn didn't care how much she protested, he wasn't abandoning her, not until he knew she was truly safe. With a nod, he stepped into the hallway to give her space. He wouldn't go far. She was fighting him with what little strength she had left and he didn't want to upset her further.

But it was his duty to make sure she was okay. He'd assigned himself her protector after the first rescue for many reasons, the least of which being a request made by her dying husband: *Take care of Billie. She deserves so much better.*

No one knew about the dying man's plea. Quinn didn't even tell his own brother, Alex.

Quinn would never forget the look in Billie's brown eyes when she was told her husband had died. It wasn't simply grief, it was complete and utter confusion. She'd obviously loved her husband and had been devastated by the loss.

After she came to work for Quinn and he got to know her better, he suspected something else, as well: regret. What he never figured out was if she regretted not being able to prevent her husband from spiraling into depression, or if she regretted marrying Rick Bronson in the first place.

"Wishful thinking," he muttered.

It would make things so much easier if Quinn thought she'd wanted out of her marriage long before her husband died. Easier as in easier to pursue something more than friendship with Billie? *That's not easy. That's insanity.*

He'd made himself a promise never to go there with her, no matter how much his heart ached to have this special woman in his life. He simply didn't deserve that kind of goodness, and she surely deserved better than a blackguard like Quinn.

"Quinn?"

Quinn spotted his friend Aiden with his sister, Bree, heading in his direction. The tall, sandy-haired Aiden had become a good friend after they'd met on a search-and-rescue mission a few years ago. They'd bonded over their military service and love of hiking.

"Hey, man, thanks for the call," Quinn said as they shook

hands. He never would have made it to Billie as quickly as he had if Aiden hadn't called him. "Hi, Bree."

"Oh, Quinn, I'm so sorry. I got here as soon as I could." She hugged him and Quinn glanced at his friend, questioning the emotional moment. Aiden shrugged.

"How is Billie?" Aiden asked.

"Banged up and cranky."

"Billie, cranky?" Bree said, breaking the hug. "She must be hurting."

"She's putting on a good front, playing tough. But I sense she's in a dark place."

"And probably not only because of the fall," Bree said.

Quinn studied her for a second, trying to figure out the meaning of her words.

"We've become friends," Bree explained. "So I know a lot about her past, her marriage, stuff like that."

Quinn wondered what "stuff" she knew about him.

"I'm so glad she activated the locator beacon and I got the emergency text," Bree said. "She almost didn't get the device, but I insisted."

Quinn studied the twenty-seven-year-old search-and-rescue K9 team member. "Did you know she was going into the mountains by herself?"

"I did," Bree said.

"Why did you let her go alone?"

"She's an experienced hiker," Bree offered. "She knew what she was doing."

"That's not the point," Quinn said.

"Billie is a grown woman. She's not your little sister," Bree said. "She's extremely capable. She's joined the SAR team and last month helped locate an Alzheimer's patient who went missing."

"I didn't know that."

"She said you two hadn't spoken in months. Anyway, she needed to go into the mountains for—"

"Closure, I get it," he said, a little impatient.

"Really, Quinn? Because I doubt you've ever sought closure for any of your brief relationships."

"Bree," Aiden warned.

Her sharp words stung, but were not untrue.

"I'm going to see Billie." Bree brushed past the men and went into the E.R. examining area.

"Sorry, man, she can be snappy when she's worried about a friend," Aiden said.

"It's okay, I probably deserved it."

"A few SAR members have been texting me about Billie, wanting to know if they can visit, bring flowers or something."

"Maybe when we get her home. Right now she needs peace and quiet."

"So, what happened? She's a solid hiker."

Quinn looked at Aiden. "She was assaulted."

"What?"

Quinn led Aiden to a visitor waiting area where they could speak privately. "Some guy on the trail threatened her. In an effort to get away it seems she fell off the trail."

"She must have been terrified," Aiden said.

Quinn's gut clenched at the thought. "She's not safe, not until we find out what her husband was into."

"My cousin Tyler is a sheriff's deputy. Want me to call him?"

"No, Officer Vanguard already took her statement, but thanks."

"Are you staying with her?"

Quinn glanced down the hall toward the examining area. "Yes, even if I have to camp outside her hospital room."

"You should ask to stay in her room tonight," Aiden suggested.

"She'd never allow it." Quinn glanced at his friend. "I think it's a pride thing."

"Well, someone's got to stay with her. Maybe Bree can stay."

"No. I don't want to put your sister in danger."

"You think it's that bad?"

"I won't know what to think until I have more information. I need to get my clothes and laptop from the car. Can you hang out here for a few minutes and keep watch?"

"Sure. Go ahead, I'll check in on Billie."

Aiden walked away. Quinn didn't move for a few seconds. Even in a hospital full of doctors and nurses Quinn worried about Billie's safety.

Now he was overreacting. Her attacker wouldn't wander into a hospital to do her harm. She could identify him since she'd seen his face.

Which only put her in more danger.

Quinn headed to his car, focusing on the next three steps to achieve his goal. His organized mind had served him well, both in business and the military. He'd created the term *the next three* to help his staff stay focused on the prioritized projects of the day.

In staff meetings he'd remind everyone about the importance of focus, yet today his focus had been blown to bits the second he saw Billie's still body lying on the plateau below the trail.

Jogging to his car, he reminded himself that Aiden was a capable man and between him and hospital security, no harm would come to Billie in the next ten minutes, the time it would take Quinn to change clothes.

Quinn had been very appreciative when Aiden offered Billie a job at Echo Mountain Resort months ago. Aiden said the favor was the least he could do considering Quinn designated the barn on the resort property as Search and Rescue headquarters for folks in their part of the county.

Even though Quinn owned the resort, he rarely meddled in Aiden's management of the business. Sure he'd hoped

Aiden would hire Billie. She needed to get away from Quinn and their dysfunctional relationship to start a new life, which she had as a hostess for the resort's four-star restaurant. Quinn knew firsthand what a gracious hostess Billie could be since she'd planned plenty of dinners for Quinn and his business associates.

But those weren't the only people he'd entertained at his lake house, and whenever he'd bring a woman to his place, Billie would serve a four-course, delicious meal. She'd smile and explain what ingredients were in the dishes she was about to serve, a smile that never seemed to reach her eyes.

Every time he brought home a date he sensed he was breaking Billie's heart, even though he'd been clear that he and Billie could never be more than friends.

Quinn got his duffel out of the trunk and slammed it shut. He'd never meant to hurt her. Subconsciously he'd brought dates to the lake house so Billie would see what a jerk he was and keep her emotional distance.

Instead she'd always looked at him with those compassionate eyes that saw straight through to his soul.

"The next three things," he reminded himself.

He'd change clothes, contact his P.I. friend, Cody, about digging into Rick Bronson's accounts and find a quiet spot to do some work close to Billie's room.

Because there was no way he'd let anyone hurt her again.

Spending the night in a hospital was dreary to say the least. It was nearly midnight and Billie lay wide awake, alone and disappointed: in Rick for making bad choices, in herself for not admitting the truth sooner about their failed marriage and…

She was disappointed in Quinn.

There, she admitted that she'd secretly hoped he would have stayed close to keep an eye on her even though she'd demanded he leave.

"Talk about mixed messages," she whispered to herself.

A young, blond nurse breezed into her room. "Hi, Billie, I'm nurse Beth. Sorry I'm running late for the eleven-o'clock vitals check."

"No problem. My dance class doesn't start for another hour," she joked.

Nurse Beth smiled. "How's the pain on a scale of one to ten?" She took Billie's pulse.

"About a four. I'm basically sore all over."

"Are your ribs worse than they were this afternoon?"

"Not really."

"Good." Nurse Beth took Billie's temperature. "A-okay."

A male orderly in his mid-twenties with coal-black hair brought a wheelchair into the room. "Doctor wants another CT scan."

"I didn't see that order," Nurse Beth said.

The orderly handed her a piece of paper.

"Huh, okay." She looked at Billie. "Let me help you."

Nurse Beth helped Billie slide out of bed. A little light-headed, Billie plopped quickly down into the wheelchair.

"Take good care of her," Nurse Beth said, hooking the IV bag to the wheelchair.

"Will do."

The orderly pushed her out of the room and down the hall to the elevator. Although she'd been unable to sleep in her hospital bed, she felt drowsy from the meds they'd given her to manage the pain.

"So, head injury, huh?" the orderly said, pressing the down button on the elevator.

"And ribs and wrist. I decided to tumble down a mountainside for fun."

"Whoa."

"So, what's your name?" she asked.

"Dylan."

"I'm Billie."

"Nice name."

"Thanks."

He wheeled her into the elevator and the doors closed.

"Needless to say, I won't be hiking for a while," she said.

"I used to love to hike."

"Used to?"

"No time. I work at the hospital, plus go to community college and help out with the family business."

"Which is…?"

"Restaurant."

"What kind?"

The elevator doors opened to the imaging department.

"It's called Healthy Eats. Sustainable living, organic ingredients, stuff like that."

"Oh, I heard about that opening up. Interesting concept."

"Yeah, Mom had some health issues a few years ago so she and Dad changed our entire menu to be more health oriented."

"So no cheeseburgers, then?"

"Sure, but we use grass-fed beef," he said.

He wheeled her into the imaging room for the CT scan and looked around. "Huh, the tech was supposed to be waiting for us. You okay here for a second? I'll go find him."

"Sure."

He locked the wheels and went in search of the technician. She studied the CT machine, which looked like a large doughnut. That thought made her tummy grumble and she realized she hadn't eaten anything substantial since breakfast.

"Hey!" a male voice shouted.

A crash echoed in the hallway.

She heard grunting and a squeak, like rubber soles kicking against vinyl flooring.

The hair bristled at the back of her neck.

It couldn't be what it sounded like. No, low blood sugar

was sending her imagination into overdrive. Dylan would be back shortly with the tech and everything would be fine.

Her gaze darted to the wall phone. If she'd learned anything from being married to Rick, it was to listen to her gut.

Billie grabbed her IV bag off the hook and shuffled to the wall, grabbed the phone—

A pop resounded from the hallway, then silence. She frantically pressed buttons, trying to focus, trying to press the right button to call security, the operator, someone who could help her.

Suddenly the lights went out, plunging her into complete darkness.

THREE

Quinn had done a pretty good job of maintaining his distance while keeping an eye on Billie's hospital room. Luckily he'd been able to convince the nurse to let him stay close by, explaining that he was worried about Billie's safety.

Which is why he didn't like having to go outside to take a business call. But there was a crisis at Decker's Resort and he had to find a solution before guests were inconvenienced. Being a closet computer genius, Quinn talked the manager through a couple of troubleshooting protocols and they got the system up and running again.

Although he'd done his best to keep the call brief, it had taken half an hour to resolve the issue. As he headed into the hospital, he decided to take a chance and peek into Billie's room for peace of mind. She'd surely be asleep by now so it would be safe to check in on her without being caught. Maybe that would ease the knot in his chest.

He wandered down the hall, stepped into her doorway and froze. The bed was empty. Her sheet and light blanket were crumpled into a ball at the foot of her bed.

Fighting the panic gnawing at his gut, Quinn strode to the nurses' station.

"I still think it's a mistake," a middle-age nurse said to a young blond nurse.

The blond nurse handed a piece of paper to her counterpart. "Maybe scheduling meant 11:45 a.m. not p.m."

"Excuse me," Quinn interrupted. "I'm looking for the patient in room 210?"

"An orderly took her to imaging," the blond nurse offered.

"Give her a minute. She'll be right back," the other nurse said.

"It takes more than a minute," the blond nurse countered.

"I'm telling you, it's a mistake. Dr. Green wanted her to get a good night's sleep. He wouldn't have ordered a scan in the middle of the night."

"Well, somebody ordered it," the blonde said.

"Probably for tomorrow." The older nurse typed something into the computer and frowned. "Huh."

"What?" Quinn asked.

"I see the scan request for tonight, but I have no idea who ordered it. I've never seen this doctor's name before."

"Where's imaging?" Quinn said.

"Basement."

Quinn took off.

"Down the elevator to the left," the blonde called after him.

He didn't have the patience for the elevator. He took the stairs two at a time and swung open the door to the basement level.

Pitch blackness greeted him. Instincts on full alert, he pulled out his smartphone and clicked on its flashlight application. Fighting to calm the adrenaline pouring through his body, he aimed the light down the hallway, slowly making his way to imaging.

The deafening silence spiked panic in his chest as he took slow, determined steps. Then he had a thought: if someone was down here planning to harm Billie, Quinn's very presence could scare him off. "Billie?" he called out.

Silence. A pit grew in his stomach. Had the attacker already found her? Hurt her?

"Billie, answer me!" he demanded.

"Quinn?" her soft voice drifted down the hall.

"I'm here." He headed in the direction of her voice and turned the corner. He spotted a man dart out of a room and race down the hall.

Quinn wanted to go after him, but needed to get to Billie. As he approached the doorway he spotted something on the floor: a body. He knelt beside an unconscious young man in scrubs and placed two fingers to his neck. Luckily his pulse was strong and steady.

The slam of a door echoed down the hall.

"Quinn? Are you there?" Billie's shaky voice called from inside the room.

"Right outside the door," he said.

"What happened?"

"You'll be okay, buddy," he whispered to the orderly. He stood and aimed the beam of his phone into the room, but couldn't see Billie. "Where are you?"

She peeked her head around the CT machine. He'd never seen her eyes so big and round before, not even the day they'd rescued Billie and her husband from the mountain.

No, tonight her expression read utter fear.

He crossed the room, knelt beside her and pulled her against his chest. She let out a gasp, like she'd been holding her breath.

"It's okay. I'm here." He stroked her hair, holding her close. Relief finally uncoiled the knot in his chest.

She placed her hand against his chest and leaned back to look into his eyes. "Dylan went to find the tech but didn't return."

"Twentyish kid with short black hair?"

"Yeah."

"He's okay, but unconscious. Is there a phone in here?"

"On the wall." She pointed.

He handed her his smartphone. "Aim the light toward the phone and I'll call security."

She pointed the beam of light and Quinn found the phone

hanging off the cradle. He grabbed it, pressed zero and waited.

Billie was okay. Everything was going to be fine. The knot in his chest might have uncoiled, but tension still hummed through his body.

Billie had been threatened, in danger, and where was Quinn? Absent. He'd abandoned her. More proof of his deep-seated failure.

"Operator," a woman answered.

"My name is Quinn Donovan. The lights in the basement are out and someone was attacked. Notify security and turn on the emergency lights, please."

"Who is this?"

"Quinn Donovan. My friend is a patient here, Billie Bronson. Send someone with a stretcher to the basement. One of your orderlies was knocked unconscious." Quinn hung up and turned to Billie. "We're going to be fine."

As Billie nodded with relief, a tear trickled down her cheek. His chest ached at the thought of her being terrorized.

"Come on, let's get you in the wheelchair." He helped her stand. She wavered and he automatically picked her up.

"What are you doing?" she said.

"I don't want you to fall down and hit your head again."

She pointed the smartphone to illuminate his way and he carried her across the room to the wheelchair. The emergency lights popped on with a click.

Which only made matters worse since now he could really see how terrified she was. Her cheeks were flushed and her eyes continually scanned her surroundings. Then her gaze landed on the doorway where the orderly lay unconscious.

"Dylan," she whispered.

"He's okay," Quinn assured.

"But—"

"Billie, look at me." With his thumb and forefinger he

tipped her chin so she'd look into his eyes. "Dylan's okay. You're okay. Everything's going to be fine."

Quinn had meant it when he told Billie everything was going to be fine. Unfortunately the hospital security guard was on a power trip and Quinn was the victim of the guy's overblown ego.

"So you mysteriously happened to know your girlfriend was in trouble?"

"She's not my girlfriend. I guessed she was in trouble when I heard the nurses talking about the mysterious doctor who'd ordered the CT scan."

"Is she a former girlfriend?" the security guard pushed. His nametag read Steven and he looked to be in his forties.

"She's a friend," Quinn clarified.

Steven walked to the corner of the small office and crossed his arms over his chest. "How do you know each other?"

"Do you have someone watching her room?" Quinn asked. "Because she might still be in danger."

"You didn't answer my question."

"I was on the rescue team that recovered Billie and her husband a year ago."

"And you kept in touch? Isn't there a name for that? Some kind of syndrome or something?"

"She fell on tough times and I gave her a job and a place to live after the accident."

"With you?"

"What's with all the questions?"

"Why are you afraid to answer?" Steven pushed.

"I'd rather be watching over my friend."

"Don't worry. She's fine."

Quinn leaned back in his chair. "You're enjoying this, aren't you?"

"What?"

"Pretending to be a real cop."

Steven took a step forward and gripped the metal flash-light on his belt. Quinn's older brother always said Quinn should learn to control his smart mouth. But right now Quinn couldn't control it because he was worried about Billie. Well, he wasn't going to get back to her if he kept antagonizing this guy.

"That was outta line," Quinn apologized.

The door swung open and a rugged-looking, middle-age man in a crisp navy suit joined them. He glanced at Quinn, then at the security guard.

"Hey, Steve." The men shook hands. "Could you go re-lieve Officer Trent outside Mrs. Bronson's room?"

"Sure." Without looking at Quinn, Steve left and shut the door behind him.

"So you're the infamous Quinn Donovan?" The guy slapped a folder onto the table.

"I don't know about infamous, but yeah, I'm Quinn Don-ovan."

"Detective Issacs, Echo Mountain P.D. Good to meet you." The guy extended his hand.

Quinn must have look skeptical.

"Relax, I know your brother, Alex." They shook hands. "We worked on a task force together a few years ago. When Steve gave me your name I made the connection and gave your brother a call to confirm." Detective Issacs sat across the table from Quinn. "So, give me your take on what hap-pened to Mrs. Bronson."

"I think someone's after her. You know about the assault on the trail, right?"

Issacs nodded. "Officer Vanguard filled me in. Mrs. Bronson thinks it has something to do with her husband's criminal activity?"

"She does."

"What was he into?"

"We're not sure."

Detective Issacs opened a folder and glanced at its contents. "I did a background check on Rick Bronson. He moved from Idaho to Echo Mountain five years ago for a job at—"

"Evergreen Lumber, I know."

"So you knew the Bronsons back then?"

"Actually, no." After the accident Quinn had discovered that Billie's husband had worked for a company Quinn and his partners shut down due to mismanagement and lack of productivity.

Another reason Quinn felt responsible for Billie's situation after her husband had died. It was becoming obvious to Quinn that being unemployed and broke had motivated Rick Bronson to pursue questionable sources of income, which meant Quinn was responsible for Rick Bronson's desperation, Billie's failed marriage and, yes, even her current predicament.

"Maybe Mrs. Bronson should get out of town, stay with relatives," Detective Issacs suggested.

"She doesn't have any."

"No parents or siblings?"

"No, sir. She's alone."

"Well, she's got you. That's a plus. Your brother told me about your military background. You'll make the perfect bodyguard."

"She doesn't want me around, requested I stay out of her room. Didn't Steve tell you? That's why he was giving me a hard time and considered me a suspect."

"Well, maybe she's had a change of heart since the attack in the imaging department. Your timing couldn't have been better."

"Tell me about it." Quinn fisted his hand. If he'd shown up a few seconds later…

"I don't think it's wise for her to go to her place when she's released," the detective said.

"I agree. I have some ideas on that."

"I'll dig into Rick Bronson's background and you take care of his wife."

There's nothing Quinn would like better than to take care of Billie…if she'd let him.

"I'd like to hire a P.I. friend of mine to look into things, if you're okay with that," Quinn said.

"Sure, as long as you share your information."

"Will do."

When Billie was admitted to the hospital after yesterday's fall, she was determined to distance herself from Quinn, yet she'd actually slept a few hours last night thanks to Quinn staying in her room. He wouldn't take no for an answer.

Every time she'd wake up, she'd catch a glimpse of him sitting in the corner working on his laptop, and the clicking sound soothed her to sleep.

Well, that and his masculine presence, strong and determined, acting as her protector. She had to admit she liked having someone looking out for her, although she knew better than to get used to it.

A nurse came in to take her vitals at 6:00 a.m.

"Good morning, I'm Nurse Rose," she said, then noticed Quinn in the corner. "Oops."

Quinn's eyes were actually closed, and his head tipped back as he dozed.

"Sorry," Nurse Rose whispered.

"I'm awake." Quinn shifted in his chair and rubbed his eyes.

It amazed Billie how he could look like a strong and powerful man one minute and a little boy the next. Billie always suspected a wounded little boy lived inside Quinn's grown-up body.

Dr. Green came into the room and stopped at the foot of Billie's bed, analyzing a chart. "Heard there was a little excitement last night."

"And here I thought hospitals were supposed to be quiet. I want my money back," Billie teased.

Quinn cracked a slight smile.

"I don't blame you," Dr. Green said. He directed his attention to the nurse. "Vitals are...?"

"Good."

Dr. Green glanced at Billie. "Your pain level, on a scale of one to ten?"

"Two."

"Billie, it's the day after a fall," Quinn challenged. "You've got to be hurting more than a two."

"Fine, it's more like four. But I really want to go home."

"There's nothing to indicate anything more serious than the slight concussion and bruised ribs. No broken bones or internal damage." The doctor glanced at her over his reading glasses. "It's quite remarkable considering what you've been through."

"So, I can go?"

"I'll sign the release papers and your husband can take you home." He nodded at Quinn, who went completely white.

"No, he's just a friend," Billie corrected.

"Well, friend—" the doctor turned to Quinn "—Billie should be ready to go in about an hour."

"Thanks." Quinn closed his laptop and gathered miscellaneous papers.

He seemed nervous at the mere mention of being Billie's husband. Well, he didn't have to worry. She'd tell him so the minute they left the hospital. And take her where? It probably wasn't safe to go to her apartment.

The doctor gave the nurse instructions and smiled at Billie. "Limit your activity for the next three to five weeks. Lie around, watch TV, read a book."

"What about work?"

"Aiden can find someone to cover for you," Quinn said.

"I'd hate to leave him shorthanded," she countered.

"What is your line of work?" the doctor asked.

"I'm a hostess at the Echo Mountain Resort restaurant."

"Is there a lot of bending and lifting involved?" the doctor asked.

"Not really. I mostly seat guests and sometimes bus tables."

"I'd rather you not lift anything," the doctor said. "The nurse will give you the rest of my instructions."

"Thanks."

With a nod, the doctor left the room.

Billie eyed Nurse Rose. "How's Dylan, the orderly who took me downstairs last night?"

"A nasty bump on the head, but he's fine. These kids are tough." She smiled.

Billie felt guilty that she'd indirectly been responsible for his injury.

"Let's go over a few things for your recovery," the nurse said. "Keep the wrist wrapped tight for a week to ten days. Then you can take off the wrap and see how it feels."

"What about the ribs?" Billie shifted and winced against the pinch in her chest.

"Ice the area for twenty minutes, four times a day to help them heal. You can wrap them if it feels better, but not too tight. The tendency is to take shallow breaths but you want to try to avoid that."

"Okay, sure. How do I wrap my ribs?"

Nurse Rose pulled a compression bandage off a nearby cart and glanced at Quinn. "I need to show her how to wrap her ribs."

"Okay." Quinn didn't move.

The nurse glanced at Billie in question.

"I should watch so I can help her," Quinn said.

"Oh, I don't think so," Billie said.

"But—"

"No," Billie said. The thought of him touching her with gentle, nurturing hands made her crazy. "Please give us some privacy, Quinn."

Without another word of protest, Quinn left the room. Billie must have seemed unusually tense because the nurse studied her. "You okay?"

"Yeah, thanks."

At least she would be as soon as she got to work on a plan to protect herself, not only from Rick's shady business associates but also from relying too much on Quinn Donovan. In her wounded state it wouldn't take much to surrender and let him take the lead, especially after he'd saved her last night.

That's what the old Billie would have done. Handing her life over to a man is what she'd done with Rick. She'd trusted him to support her and take care of her and look how that turned out.

Never again. She'd learned that painful lesson and didn't plan on repeating it.

It was midafternoon before Billie was officially discharged. As Quinn steered his SUV to the hospital entrance, he spotted her being wheeled out by a volunteer. Quinn could tell she shivered against the cool, misty rain. He wished he could hold her and warm the chill from her body.

A dangerous thought, Donovan.

He got out of the car and came around to help her but she waved him off. "I'm good."

Once she was safely buckled, he got behind the wheel and prepared for battle. She wasn't going to like his plan, but somehow he had to convince her it was the best way to keep her safe. He pulled out of the hospital lot and headed east.

"This isn't the way to my apartment," Billie said, glancing out the window.

"We're not going to your apartment. I've made other arrangements."

"No, I can't go to the lake house," she said in a panicked voice.

"No worries," Quinn said. "I'm not taking you home with me."

Quinn's chest ached. She seemed horrified by the thought of going to Waverly Harbor and staying in the coach house on his property. Had it been such a bad five months? It hadn't been for Quinn. Seeing her at least once a day had always brightened his mood.

That was then. Today he had to respect her need for distance. He knew she was wise to feel this way.

"I think it's best if I move away," she said.

He clenched the steering wheel. He suspected she wouldn't share the forwarding address with Quinn.

"To where?" he asked.

"I don't know." She glanced out the window. "Someplace safe where I can hide out and investigate this mess."

"Moving is exhausting. You need to rest and take care of yourself."

She scoffed.

"What?" he said.

"That sounds weird coming out of a guy's mouth."

"I'm sure it's not the first weird thing I've said."

"True." She smirked.

At least it wasn't a scowl.

"Billie, you need time to recuperate from your fall. I'm going to make sure you do just that."

"I'll rest better in my own bed."

"That may be true, but your apartment is the first place someone will look for you."

"'Someone,'" she sighed. "I wish I knew who 'someone' was."

"I'm working on it."

She glanced at him in question.

"I've hired a private investigator to look into things," he explained.

"I asked you not to do that. I can't afford—"

"He's a friend and he owes me a favor, okay?"

"Okay." She shifted slightly, wincing against the pain of bruised ribs.

His gut twisted when she did that. He wanted to ease her pain somehow, yet knew there wasn't a lot you could do about bruised ribs but let them heal on their own.

"We'll ice the ribs as soon as we get there," he said.

"Where are you taking me?"

"You've got a suite at Echo Mountain Resort."

"I can't afford those rooms."

"I own the place, remember?" He winked.

"But Aiden needs the rooms for real guests."

"They're not even at half capacity, plus they've got a solid security system and plenty of activity. Even if the guy finds out where you are, he wouldn't risk making a move on you in a busy setting like that."

She sighed. "I guess, if that's my best option."

"It is, in my opinion."

"You'll drop me off and head back to Waverly Harbor?"

He hesitated before answering. "I know you want me to say yes, but I can't."

"Why not?"

Talk about a loaded question.

"I need to make sure you're okay," he said.

"Because I'm still your wounded-bird project?"

"Don't say that."

"Or is it because you feel guilty?"

He clenched the steering wheel, but didn't answer. He had plenty to feel guilty about, from taking away her husband's income by closing the plant to letting her develop an attachment to Quinn when he knew it wasn't real.

"You don't have to feel guilty about anything, Quinn. I was fragile when I first went to work for you, but I'm different now and I can stand on my own two—"

A bump from behind made Billie yelp.

He'd been distracted by their conversation and hadn't noticed a car following way too close. Eyeing the rearview mirror, he considered speeding up but didn't want to put them both at risk by going too fast for conditions and spinning off the road.

The car retreated and flashed its lights.

"Does he want us to stop?" she said, eyeing the side mirror.

"That's not happening."

The car smacked into them again. Billie lurched forward and groaned against the pain in her ribs.

Quinn handed her his phone. "Call 9-1-1."

She focused intently on the phone and made the call. "My name is Billie Bronson," she said. "We're on Route 2 and someone is trying to run us off the road."

Quinn again glanced at the car in his rearview mirror. It dropped back even farther. Not good.

"Tell them we've been working with Detective Issacs," Quinn said.

He glanced into the rearview and noticed the car speed up.

"Billie!" He instinctively threw his arm across her body to brace her.

The other car clipped Quinn's bumper.

Quinn spun the wheel to avoid careening into a ditch. He tapped the brake but lost control as they skidded into a full spin.

FOUR

Billie held her breath, praying the SUV would stop before they crashed into something. Eyes pinched shut, she struggled to breathe against the nausea filling her stomach. She clenched her jaw in frustration. After everything she'd been through she did not want to die this way, in a tangle of steel and rubber, lying on the side of the road.

That's when she felt the pressure of Quinn's firm arm across her chest, as if somehow he thought brute strength could protect her. She didn't mind the connection, didn't mind feeling connected to something.

He ripped his arm away and she heard him twist the steering wheel one way, then the other, as a soft grunt escaped his throat.

A few seconds later, they broke free of the spin and she cracked open her eyes. They were cruising at a safe forty-five miles per hour down the highway.

She gasped a breath of air. "We didn't crash."

"I didn't want the airbags to go off. It would have aggravated your ribs."

She couldn't believe that her bruised ribs were his primary concern. "Did you get the license plate of the car?"

Quinn shot her a quizzical look.

"What?" she said.

"You're being awfully pragmatic about this. I thought you'd be more freaked out."

"I can freak out later. Right now I'm angry."

"Sorry, I didn't catch the plates. It was a late-model Ford truck, dark blue or black. We'll call it in when we get to the resort."

"Why wait?"

"I thought you might need a few minutes to catch your breath. I know I do," he said under his breath.

She watched his eyes dart between the rearview mirror and the road ahead of them. He was acting calm, but she sensed his worry.

"Do you think they followed us from the hospital?" she asked.

"Don't think so. I would have noticed someone following me that long."

"Which means they know your SUV and were looking for you?"

"Let's not jump to conclusions. For all we know it could be—"

"Don't say it."

"What?"

"That it could have been a random fender bender. That's too much of a coincidence, Quinn."

"Let's get to Echo Mountain Resort and call the police. We can speculate later."

With a nod, she leaned against the seat. If she wasn't safe with Quinn, that meant...

She wasn't safe anywhere. Her mind started spinning and her heartbeat hammered against her chest. She hated feeling so vulnerable and helpless.

Wasn't it enough that she'd been married to a man with a volatile temperament, that she'd walked on eggshells half the time, never knowing if he'd be in a good mood or sour one on any given day?

She ached for stability and peace. She closed her eyes and fought the fear flooding her chest. *Please, God, help me find peace.*

"Billie?"

She snapped her attention to Quinn, whose forehead was creased with worry.

"I'm okay," she said.

She wouldn't let worry cloud her judgment, not with her life at risk, and Quinn's. Although she and Quinn could never be a couple, she wished the best for him, hoped he'd eventually develop a relationship with God and find a kind and loving woman with whom to share his life.

"It could have been a random thing," Quinn said. "Someone dealing with an emergency, or a guy who had one too many beers after work."

"They would have stopped to exchange insurance information."

"Not necessarily." He glanced at her. "Sometimes it's too hard to face your mistakes."

Why did she get the feeling he was referring to himself? She glanced out the passenger window, finally taking a slow, deep breath.

"So, how do you like working at Echo Mountain Resort?" he asked.

She turned to him. "What?"

"The resort? What's it like working for Aiden McBride?"

"It's great. He's very respectful of his employees."

"That's good to know. Did he ever tell you about our first search-and-rescue mission together?"

She realized this was Quinn's attempt to take her mind off the immediate danger.

"No, he didn't."

"It was four, maybe five years ago. I was new and got assigned to Aiden's team. Two kids got separated from their group and no one noticed. They were thirteen and there was speculation that they'd intentionally run away, but Aiden ignored the possibility and had the team fan out just like any other rescue mission."

"Why's that?" She leaned against the headrest and studied his profile. He was a handsome man, but never acted arrogant about his looks.

"Aiden knew the parents of the one kid and thought highly of them. He couldn't believe their child would run away from loving parents."

"But you weren't so sure?"

"People aren't always what they seem on the outside. Justin's dad might be great to go kayaking with, but that didn't mean he was father-of-the-year material. The mom was very involved with her kids' school and church activities, but again, you never know what goes on behind closed doors."

"Speaking from experience?" she pressed.

"Yeah, well..." He shrugged. "Aiden's determination to find these kids saved their lives. Other folks weren't that concerned because the kids had been talking about running away, living in an abandoned barn. You know how kids talk. So a group of adults called neighboring farms, friends in the area, and searched empty properties."

"But Aiden didn't buy it?"

"It's like he instinctively knew they were in trouble in the mountains and wasn't giving up."

"He had faith."

Quinn hesitated, then continued his story. "Aiden interviewed every kid in the group and guessed where they were headed. Apparently Justin's friend Liam twisted his ankle and couldn't walk. Justin didn't want to abandon him, and couldn't get a cell signal in the mountains, so they were stranded. Justin assumed hikers would pass by, but the weather had turned bad pretty fast so seasoned hikers weren't taking any chances."

"Those kids must have been so scared."

"They were, but sometimes..." he hesitated "...terrifying situations make you stronger."

Again, she suspected he was referring to his own life,

his own terror. She wanted to ask what happened but knew better. In the five months she'd been living on his property he'd kept his past and his secrets locked up tight inside. Another reason they could never be more than friends: the next time she loved a man she needed to know everything about him—no surprises.

"Your team found them?" she said.

"Two hours later. They were okay, but scared."

"I know the feeling."

Quinn looked at her. "You don't have to be scared as long as I'm around."

"I appreciate that Quinn, but you won't be around forever." An awkward silence stretched between them. He didn't argue the point, which meant he agreed that he wasn't meant to be a part of her future.

Quinn's phone rang and he pressed the speakerphone button on his visor. "Donovan."

"Quinn, it's Detective Issacs. I received a strange call from dispatch about you being run off the road?"

"Someone tried, but we're okay."

"Is Mrs. Bronson with you?"

"Yes. We're on our way to Echo Mountain Resort."

"I'll meet you there for the details. Where are you now? I'll send a squad car as an escort."

"We're close, about to turn off onto Mountainview Drive. We'll be fine."

"Okay, I'll see you there."

Quinn pressed the speakerphone button and glanced at Billie. "I'll give Issacs a description of the vehicle. He'll track it down and find the guy."

"What if it isn't the bearded man? What if there's more than one guy after me, Quinn?"

"The next three."

"What?"

"Focus on the next three things that have to happen. We

get you settled at the resort, we give a description to the cops and we meet with my P.I. friend. That's all you need think about right now. Don't let your mind go spinning off into worryland."

"The next three," she whispered.

A few minutes later they pulled into Quinn's special garage on the north end of the resort.

"Stay in the car." He got out and scanned the property, then came around and opened her door.

"See anything suspicious?"

"No, we're good." He offered his hand.

She hesitated before taking it, but when she shifted a spark of pain tweaked her chest.

"It's okay to let me help you," he said.

She took his hand and embraced its warmth, its strength. She got out of the car and he led her to his private entrance. He closed the garage door and guided her through a small laundry room that opened into a great room.

"This is beautiful, Quinn," she said.

"Thanks. I booked you a suite down the hall."

"What about my things?"

"Bree swung by your place for clothes."

"But what if—"

"A police officer went with her."

He motioned her through his apartment and out into the resort hallway. They paused at room 118, he swiped the keycard and opened the door. She stepped inside the suite and froze at the sight of half a dozen friends surrounded by fragrant flowers and bright balloons.

Aiden, her boss, smiled in her direction. "Welcome to your temporary home."

"Wow, this is amazing."

Bree gave her a hug. "Hope you don't mind. They wanted to come by and see how you were doing." She broke the hug and smiled at Billie. "I put your clothes in the closet."

"Thanks," Billie said, stunned that they'd cared enough to be waiting for her.

Grace Longfellow from the K9 search-and-rescue unit held out a foil-covered plate. "I made my specialty brownies for you, and monster cookies for Quinn."

"Monster cookies, huh?" Billie smiled at Quinn.

He shrugged. "My one vice."

"I doubt that," muttered Will Rankin, field team leader for Snoquamish County Search and Rescue. She sensed he wasn't one of Quinn's biggest fans.

Nia Sharpe, resort concierge, pointed to a paper grocery bag on the desk. "I assumed you'd be taking it easy for a while so I brought books and magazines."

"And I brought my charm," Harvey Underwood blurted out.

Everyone chuckled. Harvey was in his late sixties, worked security at the resort and had become somewhat of a father figure in Billie's life.

She was deeply touched that the group had stopped by to welcome her home. Well, at least what would be her home until it was safe to return to her apartment. Oddly enough, being here, surrounded by these wonderful folks, felt more like home than her one-bedroom apartment ever had.

"Let's sit you down." Quinn led Billie to a comfortable chair.

It was a lovely suite with a roomy living area, separate bedroom and kitchenette. Once seated, clutching her sprained wrist against her stomach, she smiled at her visitors. "Thank you so much. I'm really touched."

"We were worried about you," Grace said.

"I wasn't. She's tough," Harvey offered.

"Yeah, since Harvey's got us all here, he's probably hoping for an impromptu SAR meeting at the barn," Will said.

"You can never be too prepared," Harvey shot back.

The group chuckled at Harvey's usual mantra. Billie figured hanging out with Search and Rescue friends was the closest thing Harvey had to family.

Will offered her a cup of tea. "Cream, no sugar, right?"

"Yes, thanks." As Billie took it, she smiled at Will. He was a nice man, about her age, who'd lost his wife to cancer a year ago. She sensed that if he weren't still grieving, he would have asked Billie out on a date.

Quinn nodded at her tea. "Maybe you should avoid caffeine so close to bedtime."

"It's not even four o'clock," Will argued.

"I want to make sure she gets a good night's sleep," Quinn countered.

"Who are you, her mother?" Harvey teased.

She didn't like the look in Quinn's eyes. She saw that little boy again, the one she suspected had been criticized and shunned most of his childhood.

"No, he's right," Billie said, sliding her cup onto the nearby table. "A good night's sleep will help me heal quicker."

"Well, then, you might want to stay away from Grace's brownies," Harvey said. "I've had three and I can't sit still."

"It's my special ingredient that gives you energy," Grace admitted.

"Special as in…?" Harvey asked.

"Instant coffee."

"No wonder I'm ready to run a marathon," Harvey said.

"You could harness that energy and clean the barn," Will playfully suggested.

"What, and let you miss all the fun?" Harvey redirected his attention to Billie. "Seriously now, what happened out there?"

"Someone said you were pushed," Grace said.

"By a tripped-out drug dealer," Nia offered.

"Wait, what? No, not a drug dealer, at least I don't think a drug dealer."

"You shouldn't have been hiking alone," Will said.

Quinn nodded at Will. "Agreed."

"The last thing she needs is a group lecture," Bree said.

"I think she should give us a description of the man she saw on the trail so we can be on the lookout," Aiden said.

"Is it a threat to resort guests if he finds out she's staying here?" Nia questioned.

Billie felt a twinge of guilt and glanced down at the brown carpeting.

Quinn placed a hand on her shoulder, but directed his comment to the group. "There's no threat to our guests. Since Billie is in the north wing, Aiden has instructed reservations to book the rest of the resort and not assign rooms down here. I've hired security officers to watch her room 24/7. Harvey will help coordinate."

"The first one should be here within the hour," Harvey said.

"Billie, why don't you tell them what the guy looked like," Quinn said.

As Billie described the man on the trail, Quinn wandered toward the minibar and poured himself a soda. Billie's voice pitched as she described her attacker's verbal threat and Quinn fisted his hand. The thought of someone threatening such a sweet and gentle woman made him want to break something. Perhaps he'd spend an hour in the resort's workout room later to ease the pent-up frustration and anger building in his chest.

He turned and noticed Billie studying him as she retold the tale. Distancing himself from the emotions rushing through his chest, Quinn leaned against the counter and sipped his drink. Although he hated having to listen to her retell the story, it was important that this group of people have as much information as possible. They were essentially the front line that could help protect Billie from the enemy ever getting close again.

Nia was the hub of the resort, greeting guests and helping them book kayaking adventures and hiking day trips. From her post in the lobby she saw everyone who walked through the front doors. She'd report anything suspicious to Harvey.

Harvey, the security manager, not only wandered the grounds to greet guests, but he also enjoyed quiet time in his office reviewing the property's monitors that kept track of activity at the two-hundred-room resort.

Grace was known for having a keen sense about people, and Will Rankin, well, it was obvious he had a thing for Billie. Nothing would happen to her if Will was in the vicinity.

"But you're okay now." Bree rubbed Billie's arm in a soothing motion.

Bree was gentle and nurturing with her friend, but Quinn knew she had a strong, assertive side. Aiden never shared the whole story but Quinn sensed that something bad had happened to Bree that inspired her to become a karate black belt. Quinn pitied the guy who thought he could hurt Billie if Bree was around.

As Quinn surveyed the group, he felt satisfied that Aiden had put together a good team. At least if Quinn couldn't be with Billie every minute of every day, he felt confident about her friends keeping an eye on her. Well, her friends and the pricey security officers he'd hired. He'd identified a top-rated security company in Seattle composed of former military men, and hired them for an unspecified amount of time.

Maybe it was overkill, but no price was too high to keep Billie safe.

A knock at the door interrupted Billie's story.

"Keep talking. I'll get it." Quinn went to the door and opened it to Detective Issacs. "Detective."

Quinn motioned him into the room.

"Any news on Billie's attacker?" Bree questioned.

"Nothing yet. We've got a sketch circulating to other

law enforcement agencies. What's going on here?" Detective Issacs said.

"Team, this is Detective Issacs," Quinn said.

"Team?" Issacs raised an eyebrow.

"This is our BOLO team," Quinn explained. "They'll keep an eye out for anything suspicious and contact Aiden or our security manager, Harvey, and they'll call it in to you. I figured it was a good idea to have a few people in the know."

The detective went to the sliding glass doors and glanced out, probably scanning the property for signs of trouble. "As long as they don't get overzealous and take matters into their own hands."

"They won't," Aiden assured.

"Speak for yourself," Harvey muttered.

The detective turned to Harvey.

"Harvey," Billie warned. "I couldn't handle it if you got hurt because of me."

Harvey put up his hands in a gesture of surrender. "Okay, okay. I'll seek and report only."

"Good. Well, I'm here to take your statement about the accident," Detective Issacs said to Billie.

"What accident?" Aiden questioned.

"Someone tried to run us off the road," Quinn said.

"That's not good," Harvey said.

Bree continued to stroke Billie's arm. "Oh, honey."

"I'm fine," Billie said. "A little tired, but fine."

"That's our cue," Grace said, motioning everyone to leave. "The girl needs to rest."

Quinn watched as each person approached Billie and offered a comforting word before leaving.

"Since I live on the property you know you can call me day or night," Bree offered.

"Thanks."

Will gave Billie a hug. "You've got my number." He broke the hug and shot Quinn a disapproving look.

Grace squeezed Billie's hand and smiled. "The Lord is my light and my salvation."

"Thanks," Billie said.

The group filed out of the room, leaving Quinn, Detective Issacs and Billie alone. Quinn pulled a chair close to Billie's and Detective Issacs sat on the love seat. They spent the next hour rehashing the accident and discussing the threat against Billie.

"We might be able to get a paint sample off the bumper of your car, Quinn. I'll need to have it towed to the lab."

"That's fine. I can get another car."

Billie yawned. "I'm sorry. I guess the lack of sleep is wearing on me."

Quinn looked at the detective. "Is there anything else?"

"No, we're good. I'll check in tomorrow." He stood and walked to the door. "Good night, Mrs. Bronson."

Detective Issacs motioned Quinn to join him in the hallway. Quinn glanced at Billie. "Be right back."

Quinn followed the detective and shut the door. "What's going on?"

"How do you plan to protect her?"

"Twenty-four hour security officers," Quinn said.

"She'll have to leave the room sometime."

"And I'll be with her."

"You're a good friend." The detective winked. "Or is it something more?"

"No sir, nothing more. When will they come for my car?"

"Does tomorrow morning work?"

"Sure, I'll get my stuff out of it tonight."

"Until tomorrow then."

The detective walked away and Quinn leaned against the wall next to Billie's room. If the detective asked the question then Quinn must be giving off signals that he cared about Billie as more than just a friend. Had Billie noticed? Nah, she was too stressed out about staying alive to notice

Quinn's desperation to keep her safe. *Desperation* was the only word to describe it.

He swiped his keycard and opened the door to her room. She wasn't in the living area so he peeked into the bedroom. Billie was stretched out on the king-size bed. He hesitated, wanting to go to her, cover her with a blanket and turn off the lights. An ache swelled in his chest with his need to take care of this woman.

Which would only pull him deeper into a place where he didn't belong. He took a few steps backward and quickly left the room, shutting the door with a soft click. He slid down the wall and took a deep breath. He finally admitted that his brain was starting to shut down due to lack of sleep. He may have drifted off a few times last night, but he'd suddenly awakened at the slightest sound, especially Billie's slight whimpers when she'd changed positions in bed.

Quinn's phone vibrated and he eyed the caller ID.

"Hey, big brother," Quinn answered when he saw it was Alex.

"How's it going?"

"It's going."

"How's Billie?"

"Asleep. They had a little welcoming party for her. I think between all the socializing and last night's threat, she's exhausted."

"Good, let her sleep."

"Planning on it."

"Did you talk to her?" Alex pushed.

"About…?"

"Coming to stay with you in Waverly Harbor?"

"She won't. She'd rather I be out of the equation, I'm sure."

"And why do you think that is, Quinn?" Alex said in his big-brother voice.

"I don't know, Alex, but I have a feeling you're about to enlighten me."

A tall, broad-shouldered man turned the corner and headed toward Billie's room. "I've gotta go," Quinn said.

"Quinn—"

Quinn pocketed his phone and stood.

"Quinn Donovan?" the guy said.

"Yes."

"I'm Trevor Mills, Eagle Security."

"ID?"

Trevor flashed his photo ID.

"What's the password?" Quinn asked, to be sure.

"Echo four seventeen."

"Good, thanks. Billie's napping so I'll introduce you when she awakens. My apartment is at the end of the hall. I've got to take care of some things. I'll check back in twenty."

"Yes, sir."

"And I'll have someone bring you a chair."

"Thank you, sir, but that's not necessary."

Quinn wandered down the hall to his apartment and hesitated at the door. Trevor was a professional; Quinn didn't need to worry about Billie.

He glanced over his shoulder at the security guard. He stood very still outside Billie's door, his hands crossed in front.

"She'll be fine," Quinn whispered to himself and opened the door to his place.

A basket of fruit welcomed him on the kitchen counter. "Aiden." Quinn smiled and grabbed an apple on his way to the garage. He'd take this opportunity to empty his SUV for the police. Quinn hoped they could identify the car that hit them from paint that rubbed off in the collision.

He took a bite of the apple and swung open the garage door. His search-and-rescue gear was in the back, so he'd have to open the garage door in order to pull it out. He pressed the button and the door slowly rose. He took another bite of the apple and went around back to unload his gear.

Something caught his eye in the parking lot, a light flickering in an empty car. Or maybe it wasn't empty. He put down the apple and headed for the car. Instincts on red alert, he pulled out his phone to call security.

Someone suddenly tackled him to the ground. Landing flat on his stomach, Quinn struggled to suck air into his lungs. His attacker kicked Quinn and took off, but Quinn got hold of his boot and the guy tripped, hitting the ground. Quinn reached forward to grab his other foot, but the guy anticipated his move and kicked Quinn in the jaw.

Stars arced across Quinn's vision and his hands sprang free of the guy's boot. Quinn struggled to stay conscious to get a good description of the guy and his vehicle, but his attacker swung around and kicked Quinn in the stomach. Quinn gasped for air.

"Leave him!" a man called from the truck.

Quinn tried to make out the driver, but couldn't focus through the rain and the daze of being whacked upside the head. An arm snaked around his neck from behind, pressing on his windpipe.

"Don't mess with us, Donovan," a raspy voice said. "Protecting that woman will get you killed."

Quinn dug his hands into the guy's arm struggling to free himself, but the pressure was cutting off air and Quinn's ability to think clearly.

A high-pitched ringing sound bounced through his head and his last conscious thought was one of self-recrimination and regret.

He'd failed Billie.

And he drifted into the darkness.

FIVE

Billie awoke with a start. Disoriented. Panicked.

Where was she again? She glanced around the suite. Right, Quinn had brought her here for her protection.

"Quinn?" she said.

But she was alone. She was surprised she'd fallen asleep without Quinn in the room.

Panic suddenly gripped her lungs. She rushed to the door and whipped it open.

A stranger stood guard, steely-faced with ramrod-straight posture. "Ma'am, I'm Trevor, your security guard."

"Where's Quinn?"

"Mr. Donovan went to his residence. He said he'd return shortly."

"Something's wrong."

"Ma'am?"

"Quinn wouldn't have left me alone without saying something."

"You were napping."

Frustrated at her inability to persuade Trevor to help, she rushed into the room, called the operator and asked to speak with Aiden.

A few seconds later he answered. "Billie, what's wrong?"

"It's Quinn. He's not here. I'm worried about him."

"I'm sure he just—"

"Please, Aiden, can you check on him?"

"Sure. I'll send Harvey your way after he—"

"Send him now."

There was a silent moment and she wondered if she'd overstepped her bounds with her boss.

"I'll take care of it. Stay in your room," Aiden said.

"Thanks."

She hung up and paced, her cheeks flushed. She wasn't sure why she'd awoken in such a state....

An image flashed across her mind: she'd had a nightmare about Quinn being thrown off the trail into a black abyss. Her pulse raced into her throat and she gripped a thick-cushioned chair.

"It was just a dream," she whispered and felt foolish for making a big deal out of finding Quinn.

She'd have to apologize to her boss, that's for sure.

The sound of men's voices echoed through her door followed by footsteps pounding down the hallway outside her room.

In the direction of Quinn's apartment.

She rushed to her door and whipped it open. Trevor stepped into her path. "Ma'am, please stay in your room."

She peeked around him and spotted Aiden and Harvey at Quinn's door.

"What's going on?" she called.

They ignored her.

"What about the outside exit?" Aiden said.

"This is closer," Harvey answered, fiddling with Quinn's door.

Her security guard stepped in front of her. "Ma'am, please stay inside."

"I'm going down there, Trevor. You can't stop me."

"Come on, come on," Aiden said, irritated at the time it was taking Harvey to open the door.

Billie rushed down the hall, Trevor right beside her, accepting the fact he'd lost his argument that she stay in her room.

"Got it." Harvey swung the door open.

Aiden and Harvey seemed oblivious to her presence as she followed them through the kitchen and dining room. Harvey opened the door leading to the garage.

"Quinn?" Aiden called.

They filed into the garage. The outside door was raised.

Tires squealed and Billie spotted taillights speeding away.

"There!" Harvey pointed.

And that's when Billie saw it: Quinn's still body lying on the ground.

"No!" Billie ran toward him and the three men practically flanked her like secret service. She dropped to her knees beside Quinn's body. His eyes were closed and one hand rested on his chest. He'd look peaceful if it weren't for the scratches and redness on his face.

Aiden kneeled on the other side and gripped Quinn's wrist to feel for a pulse. Billie reached out and placed her hand on Quinn's chest, praying he wasn't seriously hurt.

"I got a pulse," Aiden said.

"Should I call an ambulance?" Harvey offered.

Quinn coughed and opened his eyes, blinking against the falling rain. "I'm fine," he said in a hoarse voice, and coughed again.

He sat up and Billie rubbed his shoulder.

"Think you can stand?" Aiden said.

"Yeah." Quinn stood, but seemed a bit unsteady. Aiden and Harvey helped him to the apartment.

Billie stayed close, continuing to stroke his back.

Quinn glanced over his shoulder. "What are you doing here?" He glared at Trevor. "Why did you let her—"

"I didn't give him a choice," Billie interrupted.

As the men led Quinn inside, he continued to scold Trevor. "You let a little thing like Billie get past you? What if those guys had— Uh…" He groaned as Aiden and Harvey helped him sit down on the sofa. Quinn gripped his head.

"I'll get ice," Billie said. She went into the kitchen and filled a freezer bag with ice as she listened in on the conversation.

"I didn't get a description," Quinn said. "He came at me from behind."

"What about the vehicle?" Harvey asked.

"Late-model Ford truck, I think."

Billie joined them in the living room and handed Quinn the ice pack. She figured he was still upset with her for running out there, so she kept her distance.

"Did the guy say anything?" Aiden pushed.

"He said not to mess with him." Quinn glanced at Billie, placed the ice against his head and closed his eyes. "That's it."

Billie sensed there was more, but he wasn't sharing, probably because it would upset her further. She didn't care so much about his attacker as she cared about him being okay. "You should go to the E.R. and get checked out by a doctor," she said.

"I'm fine, just a little bruised," he said.

"You were unconscious when we found you," she countered.

"I was resting."

Trevor snorted, obviously appreciating Quinn's sense of humor.

"No one else thinks he should be seen by a doctor?" She glanced at Aiden and Harvey.

"It doesn't matter what we think," Aiden said. "It matters how he feels."

"I'm frustrated," Quinn ground out. "And humiliated that he got the jump on me."

"You said he came at you from behind," Billie said.

"He did."

"Then how were you supposed to see him coming, Quinn?"

"She's got a point," Trevor said.

Quinn glared at the guy.

"Sorry," Trevor said.

"No injuries other than your face?" Aiden asked.

"And my bruised ego? Nah."

Aiden glanced at his security manager. "Harvey, check the security video for a clear shot of those guys."

He looked at Quinn. "There were two of them?"

"Yep. One in the car and one… I don't know where the other guy came from or what he was looking for."

He cast a quick glance in Billie's direction. They all knew the men were looking for her.

"I'll check the video." Shooting Billie a concerned frown, Harvey left.

"I'll secure the garage," Aiden said and nodded at Trevor. "How about you stand guard in the hallway outside of Quinn's door?"

"Yes, sir."

Trevor left the living room and Aiden went out into the garage, leaving Billie and Quinn alone. She positioned herself on the sofa next to him. Although he must have felt the shift in the cushions, he didn't look her way. His head was tipped and his eyes were closed as he held the ice pack against his cheek.

She'd never seen him like this, bruised and defeated. Quinn had the most confidence and healthiest ego of anyone she'd ever met.

"I'm sorry," she said.

His eyes opened and he lowered the ice pack to his lap. "For what?"

"I'm sorry this happened to you."

"Do not tell me you're blaming yourself for my beat down."

"I can't help it. When I saw you out there on the ground—" Her voice hitched.

He took her hand and looked into her eyes. "I'm okay. And this wasn't your fault." He hesitated. "It was mine."

"How do you figure?"

He slipped his hand from hers. "I was careless and cocky. I saw a suspicious vehicle and went after it on my own instead of calling for help. Stupid." He closed his eyes and reapplied the ice.

"If I weren't in your life you wouldn't be in this situation," she said.

"You're in my life because I choose you to be in my life."

"Oh, really?" she teased.

He cracked his eyes open and looked at her. "That sounded bad. Chalk it up to the head injury."

She touched his shoulder. "Do you think it's a concussion?"

"Nah. I've suffered my share of injuries and this isn't bad. I'll be fine." He lowered the ice bag. "It'll take a lot more than a kick to the head to hurt me."

She smiled, but felt tears forming in her eyes. No, she would not cry. Instead she stood and went to the kitchen. "I'll us make tea."

"Wait a second, I'm supposed to be taking care of you Miss bruised ribs, sprained wrist and concussion."

"It sounds like we're in a competition for who has the worst injuries."

Aiden entered the living room. "Everything's secure. The alarm's set, all's good out there. I'm heading to the office. You two okay?"

"Yeah, we're good," Quinn said.

Aiden nodded. "Next time you see anything suspicious call me, okay?"

"Don't have to tell me twice," Quinn said. "And you'll call me if you figure out who those guys were?"

"Better yet, call Detective Issacs," Billie encouraged.

"I'll keep everyone in the loop." Aiden left the apartment.

* * *

Quinn leaned against the sofa and pressed the ice against his face. He was going to look worse in a couple of days with bruises coloring his cheek. Hopefully he wouldn't run into big brother, Alex, or Quinn would be in for the lecture of a lifetime.

"This might help," Billie said.

As she carried a tray with two mugs of tea into the living room, Quinn stood. "Wait a minute, your wrist."

"It's better," she said with a smile.

"Uh-huh. Give me that." Quinn took the tray and placed it on the coffee table.

This time she sat in a chair near Quinn, but not on the sofa beside him. A better choice in Quinn's mind, since she was no longer within arm's reach. Every time the woman touched him she set off a mass of conflicting emotions in his chest.

"It's sweet sunshine white tea," she said. "I didn't know you drank anything but black tea and coffee."

"Yeah, well…" His voice trailed off. He knew white tea was Billie's favorite and it somehow comforted him to have it in his apartment.

"We need to talk about something," she said.

"Uh-oh." He reached for his tea.

"It still needs to steep for a few minutes."

"Oh, okay." He leaned back and waited.

"Go ahead, put the ice on." She motioned to his face.

"Stop stalling. What did I do now?"

"You think I'm upset with you?"

"I'm anticipating the worst."

She sighed. "Remember how I said I wanted to dig into Rick's accounts and figure out why these guys are after me?"

"Yes, and I'm starting to think your idea about relocating is a good one."

"I've changed my mind about that."

"Terrific," he said, sarcasm lacing his voice. Although a part of him wanted her to leave, become anonymous someplace and never look back, the other part knew she couldn't run from trouble like this.

How was he going to protect her?

"I've been a coward and I'm ashamed," she said.

"What are you talking about?" he said. "You're the bravest, smartest, kindest woman I know."

"I appreciate that, Quinn, but here's the truth—I grew up and moved away as soon as I could because my mother suffered from depression. I blindly ran into Rick's arms and I hid out in your guesthouse after Rick passed away. I have to stop avoiding the hard stuff and face it head-on." She stood and paced to the breakfast bar and back. "When I think about what that man did to you out there…I'm furious with myself."

"Why? You didn't kick me in the jaw." The minute he said the words, he realized he shouldn't have.

She studied him with a mix of anger and regret in her warm brown eyes. "But it *is* my fault." She started pacing again. He stood and blocked her, grabbing her arm and leading her back to the chair.

"You're making me dizzy," he said, trying to ease her tension.

She sat down and Quinn took his spot on the sofa. He knew she had more to say, so he patiently waited.

"After today—the welcome-home reception, the flowers and balloons—I realized I have a home here, a family I care about and who care about me. I will not let my husband's bad decisions and his bullying criminal friends intimidate me into distancing myself from that family. I've been keeping people at a distance for far too long." She glanced at Quinn. "I like feeling connected to people."

His heart slammed against his chest as he searched her

round, brown eyes. She couldn't mean him, could she? Because only last night she tried to get him kicked out of the hospital.

"You know what I mean?" she said.

"Yeah, I think I do. So you're okay with me being involved in your life until this case is resolved?"

"Absolutely, but I won't allow myself to grow too dependent on you. That's been my M.O.—lean too heavily on one person and then when he's gone, it all falls apart."

A not-so-gentle reminder that they both knew Quinn wouldn't stick around forever. Although she didn't realize it was for her own good, Quinn knew she deserved better. She deserved a good, honorable man with whom to share her life.

"What do you need from me?" he said.

"Treat me more like an equal and less like a fragile bird with a broken wing. Let me be a part of the fight to protect myself and my friends."

"You'll keep the security guard?"

"Sure."

"You'll share everything with me—information, memories, anything that relates to the case?"

"I will."

"You sure this is what you want? You wanted me booted from the hospital last night."

"That was, well, complicated. I was an emotional wreck. I've got things in perspective now. I'm ready to admit I need your help."

"Score one, Donovan," he said.

She smiled and his heart leaped.

She winked. "Be quiet and drink your tea."

Billie awoke the next morning a bit achy and irritable. She'd slept on and off, plagued by nightmares about being chased by a faceless man and Quinn being attacked by a group of men with baseball bats. That one awakened her with a start and she sat up in bed gasping for air, first out of fear, then from the pain of bruised ribs.

She'd showered and finished dressing when she heard a soft tap at her door. Eyeing the peephole, she spotted Quinn's bruised but smiling face. How could he be so chipper? He had to be hurting this morning after the assault last night.

Because of her. She gripped the door handle, anger coursing through her body.

"Billie?" he called through the door.

She flung it open. "Good morning."

He greeted her with an intriguing breakfast tray. "Sleep okay?" he said, going to the kitchenette and placing the tray on the counter.

"Not the best. You?"

"Same. Aiden had the cook make you a vegetable omelet. There's fruit, toast and sausage."

"Great, thanks. You're staying, right?"

Quinn shot a quick glance at the door, then looked at Billie. "Of course."

"There's only one plate… I get it. You were going to drop it and go."

"It's just…" he hesitated "…I've been up since five so I've already eaten."

"It's okay. I'm sure you have someplace to be," she said. "Go ahead, I'll be fine."

She sat at the counter, hoping he'd leave yet wanting him to stay. How was she going to keep her emotional distance from this man if she kept giving him mixed signals?

"Actually, I'm supposed to meet with my P.I. friend in a few minutes. I could have him come to your suite."

"Okay," she said, trying to act aloof. She cut into her omelet and took a bite. The delicious taste made her forget about her aching ribs for a few seconds.

Quinn called Nia at the concierge desk and told her to direct the investigator to Billie's room. Billie noticed how nice he looked in his dark blue suit, crisp white shirt and colorful tie. The tie was no doubt Quinn's personal statement. He was an astute businessman with an innovative streak.

"He'll meet us here," he said, walking toward her. "What's that look?"

"What look?" She bit into a piece of cantaloupe.

"You're looking at me funny."

"You look nice today."

He glanced sideways at her. "Thanks?"

"I meant it as a genuine compliment."

"Uh-huh," he said, like he didn't believe her. "The investigator I've hired is Cody Monroe. We met in Afghanistan."

"In the service?"

"Yep."

"And you both happen to live in Snoquamish County?"

"No, he's from Seattle."

"That's a long commute."

"I've booked him a room here. He'll be using an empty office at the resort as his home base." Quinn sat next to her at the breakfast bar. "He'll want to talk to you, ask a lot of questions about Rick. You good with that?"

"Sure." She forked her omelet. "Can you trust him?"

"Absolutely."

Someone knocked on the door. "That's probably him."

Quinn went around the corner to answer and Billie sighed, trying to convince herself that having a stranger dig into her life and marriage would help them figure out who was after her.

"Hey, buddy, good to see you," Quinn said.

"What's this? A fancy suit and tie? You almost look respectable."

"Yeah, yeah. Come meet Billie." They turned the corner. "Billie, this is Cody Monroe.

Cody was in his thirties with short, cropped hair and a boyish face.

She shook his hand. "Nice to meet you."

"Thanks. You, too."

"Want some coffee?"

"That'd be great," he said.

"I'll pour," Quinn offered.

Cody pulled a tablet complete with keyboard out of his backpack.

He set it on the counter and sat on a stool across from her. "So, Billie, you ready for some questions?"

"You don't waste any time," Quinn said.

"No, sir, not when lives are at stake."

Two hours later Quinn wasn't so sure hiring Cody had been his best idea. He was asking good but hard questions, questions Billie was starting to push back on.

"And the late nights, some nights when he didn't come home, where did you think he was?" Cody asked.

"What are you insinuating?"

"I'm trying to determine if you picked up on something and didn't realize it at the time."

"He didn't go out a lot, but when he did he said he was with friends from his former job at the plant."

"And you believed him?" Cody pushed.

"I had no reason not to believe him."

"You didn't get a sense that something was off?"

"I figured Rick was depressed from being laid off and not having a job for so long."

"Did he bring any new acquaintances to the house?"

"No, just the usual guys, Stuart and Calvin."

Cody typed on his keyboard. "Are they local?"

"Somewhat. I think Stuart still lives in Lake Stevens, about forty minutes from here."

"I'd like to speak with them. Do you have their last names?"

"Anderson is Stuart's name, but I don't know Calvin's. I'd heard he moved to Idaho after the plant closed."

"Did your husband work anyplace other than the plant?" Cody asked.

"Not regularly. We moved here for the plant job, and after he was laid off he got odd jobs here and there, but nothing consistent."

"Do you remember who hired him for these odd jobs?"

"Is it important?"

"Yes, ma'am. Men working odd, sporadic jobs are targets for criminal enterprises."

"Why's that?"

"Because these men, like your husband, are desperate."

Quinn took a slow, deep breath and wandered to the window overlooking the gardens. Rick Bronson had been desperate enough to put his life and his wife's life at risk. And that, too, was Quinn's fault.

"What's wrong?" Billie said.

Quinn glanced over his shoulder. She was intently studying him. "Me? No, nothing. Thinking about work stuff." He redirected his attention outside. It was a beautiful, sunny morning, so opposite his dark mood.

If only Quinn hadn't needed to close the plant and put people out of work. But he and his partners couldn't afford to let it function in the red due to mismanagement and a changing economy.

He'd helped many of the employees find jobs, some in other counties at one of his properties. But some locals didn't want to move and would rather accept unemployment than make a life change. Rick Bronson probably figured he'd made his life change of the decade by moving himself and Billie from Idaho to the small town of Echo Mountain, Washington. From what Billie had said, Rick Bronson blamed himself for making a bad decision in relocating for a job, and that blame transformed into depression and hopelessness.

A hand touched his shoulder. He glanced down into Billie's curious eyes. "Where are you?"

"What?"

"You're orbiting Jupiter, my friend," Cody said from the other side of the suite. "I'm headed out. Billie, the more you can remember, the better. You probably know more than you think you know."

"Perhaps."

Quinn didn't miss the tentative tone of her voice.

"I'll be back at dinnertime." Cody headed to the door.

"They've got a full menu in the resort's restaurant," Quinn said. "Flash them the card I gave you and they'll get you whatever you want."

"Thanks. You guys be careful." Cody left the suite.

Billie stood there, studying Quinn.

"What, my bruises are that bad?" he said.

"What are you thinking about?"

"Yikes, a man's worst nightmare, being caught thinking about football when his girlfriend hopes he's thinking about her."

"Were you thinking about football?"

Quinn wandered to the coffee maker and poured a cup. "No," he admitted. He glanced at her. "Why did Cody warn you to be careful? You're not leaving this room."

"Actually," she grabbed her fleece jacket off an upholstered chair. "I've blocked so much of the last year with Rick out of my mind that he thought it might be helpful to go to my old house. He said it might stimulate memories."

"No, absolutely not."

"Quinn—"

"You're safe here, in this room, with a guard right outside the door."

"Not necessarily. They know where I am so doesn't that make me a sitting duck?"

He clenched his jaw, frustrated by her sensible argument.

She closed the distance between them and touched his arm again. He simultaneously tensed and relaxed when she did that. How was that possible?

"The sooner I remember things and help Cody do his job, the quicker we can put an end to this," she said. "I feel like I'm holding things up by hiding out here. I need to be proactive about this, Quinn. I'm done living in denial and letting things happen to me, remember?"

"Yeah, but Billie—"

"Please. Support me on this. Help me become a stronger person."

It's not like he could deny her once she asked for something. Great, now who had the control in this relationship?

"We're taking security with us," he said.

"Of course."

"And you won't go anywhere without me right beside you."

"Agreed. I'll call my former landlord and see if we can get into the house today. It's about half an hour from here in Arlington Heights."

She pulled out her phone and made the call. Quinn sipped his coffee. He didn't like this plan for so many reasons. That wasn't his intellect talking—it was his heart. The last thing he wanted to do was put Billie in physical or emotional danger and he knew returning to the house she shared with Rick would be an unpleasant experience for her.

"We're in luck," she said. "I explained what's going on and Mrs. Wonderman said she's happy to help. Since the house is for sale, she gave me the code for the lockbox."

"When can we stop by?"

"There aren't any showings scheduled for today."

"Fine, let's go." Quinn wasn't thrilled with the idea of

going hunting for memories. He didn't want Billie exposing herself to the world, and he certainly didn't want her recalling painful memories from her marriage, or pleasant ones for that matter. *Ah, there's the truth.*

"You're doing it again," she said.

He motioned her toward the door. "Doing what?"

"Disappearing into your head."

"Lack of sleep makes me spacey I guess."

They opened the door and he explained to today's security guard, Joe Miller, that they were on the move. Quinn made a quick call to Aiden and requested a car since the police would impound his vehicle for evidence in yesterday's hit-and-run.

Nia had car keys waiting for him at the front desk. The staff at Echo Mountain Resort was the most efficient of any of his teams.

The security guard suggested Billie and Quinn take the backseat where tinted windows would conceal their identities.

They left the resort, Joe behind the wheel of the SUV.

"It's too quiet," Billie said.

"Joe, can you turn on the radio?" Quinn asked, although he suspected she'd prefer conversation with Quinn instead of music.

"Sure, any requests?" Joe said.

"Soft rock or country," Billie said.

Melodies of a soft rock song filled the car, and Quinn tried to relax, but couldn't. He anticipated Billie's emotional reaction when they got to the house, one that Quinn wasn't equipped to deal with.

Billie thought she ran from the hard stuff? Quinn had been running ever since his mom died and Sophia took over. Once you get in the habit of running, you never seem to be able to stop. That's why he'd bought so many properties all over the northwest and planned to expand his business down south. It would keep him on the move, which suited his lifestyle. It's not as if he was tied to anything in Washington State.

Thirty minutes later they turned off Highway 2.

"Turn right at the next street," Billie said.

Joe followed her directions and she pointed. "The blue house."

The security guard pulled in front of a gray-blue house with a for-sale sign in the yard. The front screen door was off its hinge, the grass was overgrown and there was a crack in a front window.

"It looks so dilapidated," she said. "You'd think Mrs. Wonderman would keep it up if she's trying to sell it."

"You sure you're up to this?" Quinn asked.

"Of course."

"Wait for me." Quinn got out and came around to Billie's side of the car as she opened her door. Joe stood close by, scanning the neighborhood.

The crack of a gunshot pierced the air; Billie shrieked and Quinn shoved her into the car.

"Get her out of here!" Quinn ordered the security guard. "Now!"

SIX

Billie grabbed Quinn's arm. "Get in the car."

"Let go, Billie."

"You promised you'd call for help, that you wouldn't do this alone."

"After you're safely away."

Another shot rang out. Quinn dove into the backseat and slammed the door. "Let's go!"

They peeled away from the house, adrenaline rushing through Billie's body. Quinn pulled out his phone and dialed emergency.

"Shots fired at 124 Honeysuckle Lane....No....Yes."

She focused on taking deep, calming breaths. She was okay. Quinn was okay. He'd done as she requested and gotten in the car. He was safe, not shot or beaten up or...dead.

As he spoke with the 9-1-1 operator, he glanced at her in question. Only then did she realize she was squeezing his hand. Hard. Embarrassed, she tried to pull away but he wouldn't let go.

"Yes, ma'am. Okay." Quinn ended the call. "They're sending a squad car. Anyone following us?" he asked Joe.

"No, sir. I don't mean to overstep, but the shooter didn't hit the vehicle or anything near us."

"Meaning?" Quinn pressed.

"We were clear targets. If he'd wanted to hit us he easily could have."

"He doesn't want to shoot Billie, just scare her," Quinn said.

"Well, he certainly succeeded," Billie muttered.

Quinn squeezed her hand, then frowned. "Hang on a second. Turn us around, Joe."

"Yes, sir."

"Quinn, what are you—"

"It's okay. You know I won't let anything happen to you." He glanced at the security agent. "Pull up to the corner, but wait until police arrive before you head down the street."

"Will do."

They didn't have to wait long. Within minutes both a local and county sheriff's police car had pulled up to the house. Billie, Quinn and Joe watched as the officers cautiously approached the house, guns drawn.

From this vantage point Billie had a clear view of the entire house. She spotted someone running out the back into the field behind the house.

"Quinn!" she pointed.

He pulled away from her and flung open his door. "Backyard!" he called to the officers, but they didn't seem to hear him. Quinn got out and slammed the car door.

"No!" She reached for the door and heard the locks click.

"Sorry, ma'am," Joe said. "It's my job to keep you safe."

She watched Quinn sprint down the street intersecting Honeysuckle, probably in the hopes of detaining the suspect. "What if he shoots Quinn?"

She saw Quinn catch up to the guy and they both went down.

"We've got to tell the police that Quinn's not the bad guy," she said.

Joe pulled up to the house and parked. One of the officers spun around and aimed his weapon.

"I could lose my job for this," he muttered.

"Go, go tell him what's going on, but unlock the windows so I can listen."

He did and got out of the truck, hands raised. "I'm with Eagle Security. We called it in."

"Spread 'em against the truck," the young officer said.

Joe did as ordered and the officer searched him.

"The guy you're looking for is out back," Joe said. "My employer, Quinn Donovan, went after him and we saw them go down in the field behind the house."

The officer spoke into his shoulder radio. "Check the backyard, over." He turned to Joe. "Please wait in the car, sir."

Joe got in the car and lowered his window. Billie fought the growing panic whirling in her belly. The other guy obviously had a gun and Quinn was unarmed. She clasped her hands to calm herself and said a prayer. *God, please protect him.*

A minute later, two officers escorted Quinn and a teenager around the corner. Both were handcuffed.

"Why is Quinn handcuffed?"

A black sedan parked next to their SUV and Detective Issacs got out of the car.

"Detective Issacs," Billie called from her window. "I had permission to go into my old house, but we heard gunshots and Quinn went after a man who took off into the field."

Detective Issacs glanced at the officer leading Quinn to a squad car. "I'll take care of it."

The detective went to the officer holding on to Quinn's arm and flashed his badge. She finally saw the expression on Quinn's face—clenched jaw, shuttered eyes—and almost wished she hadn't. She knew that look and it made her nervous. It meant he'd completely shut down, that he'd gone to an even darker place than usual.

During the months as his personal assistant she'd learned to read all Quinn's moods, from light and playful, to dark and distant. There was so much angst balled up in his body and she wished she could help him lessen that tension. Perhaps with God's love she could convince him to let go of his anger?

The police officer uncuffed Quinn and Detective Issacs escorted him to the SUV.

Billie flung open the door. She was about to hug Quinn, but his eyes were so cold that she hardly recognized him. No matter, he needed a hug.

She wrapped her arms around him and squeezed tight. He casually returned the hug. She wanted to hold on, but knew better. She broke the embrace and eyed the detective. "Thank you for clearing that up. Who was shooting at us?"

"A teenager who was squatting in the house, but he wasn't shooting at you. Apparently he saw some kind of rodent and decided to play exterminator," Issacs offered.

She glanced at one of the officers as he put the young man into the squad car. "Poor kid."

"Are you still up for checking out the house?" Detective Issacs said.

"I don't think—"

"Of course," she interrupted Quinn. She knew he was trying to protect her, but she wouldn't let a random shooting by a homeless teen change her course. She needed answers.

As the three of them headed for the house, Billie noticed Quinn rub his wrists, probably sore from where the handcuffs had pinched his skin.

"Why did they cuff you?" she asked.

Clenching his jaw, Quinn didn't answer.

"They were being cautious," Detective Issacs said. "I wish you would have called me before coming out here."

"We figured you had enough on your plate without us calling you every ten minutes," Quinn said. "What brought you here, anyway?"

"I was chasing a lead and heard the call. By the way, we won't need your car for forensics."

"Why's that?"

"Turns out the driver was an inexperienced kid driving on a learner's permit. He was late and got a little aggressive."

"A little?" Quinn said.

"His mom saw the dented fender and the kid confessed. She called it in. I think she wanted us to put him in lockup."

"Did you?" Billie said.

"No, but the chief gave him a lecture he won't soon forget."

They approached her old house and Billie got the key out of the lockbox. She took a steadying breath before opening the door. The subsiding adrenaline rush of the past ten minutes left her a bit drained.

"You okay?" Quinn asked in a soft, tender voice.

"Sure, fine." She swung open the door.

The empty house didn't even look familiar to her anymore. Without their furniture, artwork on the walls and knickknacks, this could be anyone's house in any random town.

"How long has it been since you lived here?" Detective Issacs said.

"About a year."

She wandered through the main room, running her hand across the rich wood mantel above the fireplace. She'd spent many a night sitting across from the fire, soothed by the orange glow of burning wood.

A discussion replayed itself in her mind. She and Rick had been brainstorming ways to pay the utility bill with only unemployment checks coming in. She'd wanted to increase her hours at the gift shop in town but Rick wouldn't allow it. As she drifted into the memory, she tried remembering indications that Rick was changing from a good man to a criminal. Nothing jumped out at her.

She wandered through the house into the kitchen, remembering the loaves of sweetbread, and dozens of cookies she'd baked for church functions. She glanced at the pantry door where she'd kept her baking supplies.

A vivid memory rushed to the surface: the night she'd caught Rick hiding in the pantry. She'd teased him at the time, accusing him of playing hide-and-seek. In retrospect, she wondered if he had been hiding something other than himself in there.

She wandered to the pantry, opened the door and ran her hand along the empty shelves.

"What is it?" Quinn said.

"Not sure."

A piece of paneling seemed a little askew and she pressed on one corner. It popped out, revealing a plastic bag of jewelry hidden in the wall. She snapped her hand back. "Detective?"

She backed out of the pantry and pointed. "This isn't mine."

With a latex glove, the detective grabbed the baggie. "Interesting. You knew this was here?"

"No, but I just remembered when I caught Rick hiding in the pantry and I thought it was strange."

"I'll take this in and run it for prints. Do you want to keep looking around?"

"I guess so."

"Billie?" Quinn touched her arm. "We can leave right now."

"No, I'd like to stay a few more minutes." She stepped away from him, feeling ashamed at being in this house with Quinn. Not because she felt as if she was doing anything wrong, but as the memories surfaced she realized what a fool she'd been to be so blind about Rick's secrets and lies. How many times had he told her he'd found an odd job on a construction project, or that he was going for pizza with Stuart to discuss job prospects? Was any of it true?

As she wandered into the living room, her gaze drifted

to a dent in the drywall. She remembered how it got there. She'd suggested Rick meet with a job counselor, he'd lost his temper and kicked the wall.

She never thought he'd hurt her physically, but his rage had definitely increased. She wouldn't leave him without a fight since she'd made a commitment, for better or worse, and she kept her promises. Billie wasn't a quitter. She'd never given up hope that she could bring Rick out of his funk.

She wondered if such optimism had been a mistake.

"Okay, let's go," she said, heading for the door.

"Hang on," Quinn said. "Detective, can you give us a second?"

With a nod, Detective Issacs went outside.

With gentle hands on her shoulders, Quinn turned Billie to face him. "What is it?"

"Nothing."

"I sense you remembered something and it upset you."

"I'm fine. Can we go?"

Instead, he pulled her close and held her so gently that she thought she might fall apart. She reveled in the embrace for half a second before remembering her goal: to develop a new kind of strength independent of a man.

She stepped away and reached for the door. "We should get in touch with Rick's friend Stuart. He knew him better than anybody, maybe even me."

She was too quiet. Quinn glanced at Billie across the backseat and wondered what she'd remembered at the house that caused her dark mood. Dark or contemplative? He couldn't be sure.

The only thing he was sure of was that her silence made him uncomfortable. He almost always knew what Billie was thinking. He never had to guess, and was rarely blindsided, like he'd been with other women.

Women who'd acted like they genuinely cared, when in fact they were usually interested in Quinn's reputation or money, much like his stepmother, who'd married Quinn's dad, spent all his money, then abandoned him when he was diagnosed with cancer.

But not before she did serious damage to Dad and Quinn's psyches. Luckily Alex had gotten out of the house by joining the army. Quinn, on the other hand, spent six years dodging verbal barbs and taking emotional beatings, simply for living in the same house as his stepmother.

He wondered why his dad hadn't fought back, hadn't defended his son. Years later Quinn realized that his dad had been blinded by Sophia's outward beauty and style. He thought that somehow it made him a better person to be married to a classy lady. Yeah, classy on the outside, ugly on the inside.

It had been a hard six years through his teens, but those years had taught Quinn the skill of hiding his feelings and developing a thick skin, so thick that even his ex-wife hadn't been able to get through to him. She chose to end their marriage, claiming she wanted all of him or nothing from him. Since he couldn't unlock the protective wall he'd built around his heart, she left him.

Yet Quinn never seemed to have a problem saying what was on his mind with Billie, and he sensed she knew what he was thinking and feeling, or at least knew when he was struggling with shame or regret.

Is that what was eating away at her? Did she feel regret about her marriage?

"It's not your fault," he blurted out.

She glanced at him in question.

"Whatever your husband did to pay the bills, he made that choice, not you."

"We were partners. I'm partially responsible."

"Billie—"

"Can we not talk about this?" she said with pleading eyes.

"Okay."

She glanced out the window. "How did you know that's what I was thinking about?"

"A good guess."

Joe turned down Stuart's street in Lake Stevens.

"Do you know what you're going to ask Stuart?" Quinn said.

"You mean besides was he involved in my husband's criminal ventures?"

"Maybe you shouldn't ask him outright like that."

"I'm kidding, Quinn."

They parked in front of a four-story apartment building and Quinn got out of the car. He came around to Billie's side, but she'd already opened her door.

As they strode up the sidewalk to the building, anxiety and hope whirled in Billie's stomach. What she wouldn't give for some answers right now. She pressed the button for unit 214. The door buzzed and they went inside.

"Hello?" a man called from above.

They climbed the stairs and turned the corner on the second floor. A tall man, about forty years old wearing jeans and a gray Washington State Cougars sweatshirt, hovered in the doorway.

"Hi, Stuart," Billie said.

"Billie, so good to see you." She and Stuart shook hands. Stuart eyed Quinn and Joe, the security guard. "Everything okay?"

"This is Quinn Donovan and Joe Miller. They're keeping an eye on me until we sort through some things."

"Come on in."

Quinn nodded for Joe to keep watch beside the door in the hallway. Billie and Quinn went inside.

The apartment was clean but disorganized, with newspapers and magazines strewn across the coffee table, and a stack of books on the dining room table with notes sticking out from various pages.

"Finding work can be a full-time job." He said in explanation. "But you didn't stop by to listen to me complain. How can I help you, Billie?"

Stuart motioned them into the living room. Stuart and Quinn sat down, but Billie wandered around, inspecting a photo on a bookshelf.

"We're interested in what Rick was doing when he wasn't looking for work." She pinned him with a serious look.

"You mean, the transportation gigs he got on the side?"

"Transportation?" Quinn questioned.

"He'd drive a truck over the border to Canada and come back the same day. Park the truck in Marshall's Scrap Yard and get a hundred bucks cash from the cashier."

"Do you know what was in the trucks?" Quinn asked.

"He said car parts."

"Did you believe him?"

Stuart shrugged. "A part of me did, but the other part..." He hesitated and shook his head. "The fact he was getting paid cash made me wonder."

"Did he recruit you to drive?" Quinn said.

"He tried, but I couldn't risk it. I was trying to get joint custody of my son, so I couldn't take any chances."

Billie pointed to a photo of Rick and Stuart in the mountains sporting wide grins. "Where was this taken?"

"Cascade Mountains east of Lake Riley. You remember—we used to go fishing?"

"Oh, right," she said.

"A friend of Rick's had a cabin up there," Stuart said. "It was a nice break from work."

"Yeah," Billie said in a contemplative voice.

"A detective from Echo Mountain P.D. might want to talk to you," Quinn said. "He's handling this investigation."

"Into what? You still haven't told me what this is about."

Before Quinn could respond, Billie said, "I was assaulted on the trail a couple of days ago and we think my life is in danger. We need to be proactive and figure out what they want before someone else gets hurt."

Quinn noted how pragmatic and calm she sounded, almost as if she was talking about someone else.

She glanced at Quinn. "Did I miss anything?"

"You covered it. Although—" he turned to Stuart "—I know this is a personal question, but I have to ask. Do you have a criminal record?"

"Not unless you count a drunk and disorderly. I was pretty messed up after losing my job and my marriage."

Quinn shoved his personal guilt aside as he spoke to yet another victim of the plant's closing.

"Where did you and Rick hang out when you'd go for pizza?" Billie asked.

"Go for pizza?"

"Yeah," Billie said. "Every Tuesday Rick would head out for pizza night with you."

"Um, sorry, Billie, but I had a work skills class on Tuesday nights. If he was going out for pizza, it wasn't with me."

A disappointed expression crossed Billie's face.

Quinn stood and shook Stuart's hand. "Thanks for your help."

"Sure, and Billie?"

She glanced at Stuart.

"I am truly sorry," Stuart offered.

"Thanks." With a troubled smile, she left the apartment.

Billie was thankful that Quinn gave her space and didn't ask too many questions during the ride to the resort. She was exhausted and flopped down for a nap the moment she returned to her room. Quinn seemed okay with that since he had business to tend to.

Perhaps the lack of rest was catching up to her, or the events of the day. Well, that and the fact that she kept discovering more lies her husband had told her to keep her in the dark. If he wasn't going for pizza with Stuart where had he gone? To meet with his thief friends? Because after finding the jewelry in the pantry, she assumed that's what he was into.

Her husband had become a common thief right before her eyes and she hadn't even noticed. How dense could a woman be?

After a long nap, Billie spent the rest of the afternoon reading and reflecting, praying for forgiveness for not being able to help Rick, and praying for strength to help authorities catch the men who were after her.

A few SAR members stopped by with dinner—Bree, Grace and of course, Will. Will was a nice guy, pleasant and caring, but Billie wasn't in a position to open her heart to anyone, not with all these conflicting emotions vying for dominance. She was angry and fearful, determined, yet sad. Until she got her emotions in order she wouldn't involve someone else in her drama.

Besides, Will wasn't Quinn.

Ugh. Where did that come from?

"You look whipped," Bree said, studying Billie.

"Yeah, and this is after a three-hour nap," she joked.

"Donovan should have known better than to run you all over the county," Will said.

"It was my idea," Billie countered, taking a bite of Grace's delicious fudge brownies.

"Did you make progress?" Bree asked.

Billie nodded. "A little, I think."

A knock sounded at the door. Bree put out her hand, signaling Billie to stay put. Will went to the door and eyed the peephole.

"Looks like a gift basket." He opened the door and took the basket from the security guard. "Thanks."

"What's in it?" Bree asked. "Chocolate? Candy? Licorice?"

"Hey, back off—that's my basket," Billie teased.

"But you'll share with your friends, right?" Bree smiled and batted her eyelashes.

Will placed the basket on the credenza. "Looks good. Would you like to do the honors?"

Billie went to the basket and analyzed its contents. "Chocolate, check. Hard candy, check." Bree stepped up beside her and reached for the cellophane. Billie playfully slapped her hand. "Nuh-uh. Card first. That's the proper way to receive a gift." Billie opened the envelope.

"Proper is overrated." Bree tugged at the ribbon holding the cellophane in place.

Billie pulled the card out of the envelope just as Bree plucked a piece of nondescript chocolate from the basket. She was like a little girl sometimes, Billie mused. Billie read the bold-faced type on the card.

Her breath caught in her throat.

You will die like your husband. Slowly and painfully. Unless you tell us where it is.

SEVEN

"Don't!" Billie batted the chocolate out of Bree's hand before it went into her mouth.

"Billie, what—"

Billie shoved the card at Bree. Will stood behind them and read over her shoulder.

"What is it?" Grace said. As if she knew it held bad news, she stayed at the table, eyes widening with concern.

"I need to find Quinn." Billie whipped out her phone and hit the speed dial.

"Forget Quinn, call the police," Will said.

"I'll do that, too, but Quinn first."

Bree stood there with a stunned expression on her face, staring at the basket. "You think…?" Her gaze drifted to the piece of chocolate on the carpeting.

"I'm calling the police," Will said.

"Here," Billie handed him the detective's business card as she waited for Quinn to answer. "Call Detective Issacs, he's the lead on the case."

Grace crossed the room, put her arm around Bree and led her to the dining table.

"Answer, Quinn," Billie muttered into the phone. Instead it went to voice mail. "Quinn, it's Billie. I got a threatening note in a gift basket. Where are you? Call me."

As Will mumbled something into the phone to Detective Issacs, Billie felt strong, as if she was keeping it together, for the most part. But when she studied her friends, traumatized by the thought of potentially being poisoned, Billie's nerves started to unravel. No, maybe she was overreacting.

She grabbed the wall phone and called the front desk.

"Operator."

"I need you to page Quinn Donovan. It's Billie Branson. Tell him it's an emergency."

"Yes, ma'am. Hold on."

Billie went to Bree and stroked her shoulder. "Hey, it's okay."

Bree eyed her. "How can you be so calm?"

"We won't find these guys by getting hysterical and letting fear make us crazy."

Bree glanced at the lone chocolate on the floor. "I could have been poisoned."

"Or I'm overreacting." Billie grabbed a napkin off the table and used it to pluck the chocolate off the floor. She set it next to the basket, out of sight. "It's probably not lethal. Killing me wouldn't get them what they want."

"Which is what?" Will said, pocketing his phone.

"I wish I knew. We found a bag of hidden jewelry at my old house, but I have no idea if that's what they were looking for."

Will put his arm around Billie. "The detective is on his way."

She appreciated the gesture, but couldn't stop the frustration from rising up her chest. Quinn had said she'd always be safe as long as he was around and yet he was missing in action.

"Ma'am," the operator said.

"Yes?"

"I'm sorry, but Mr. Donovan isn't answering his page."

Then a horrible thought struck her: What if he was in trouble?

"Page Aiden McBride for me?"

"Of course. Hang on."

Billie closed her eyes. *Where are you, Quinn? Why did you leave me?*

Oh brother. She couldn't have it both ways. She wanted to be strong and independent yet she panicked when she couldn't find Quinn?

She feared that the only reason Quinn would leave her was to pursue something regarding the case, which would definitely put him in danger.

She turned to her guests. "And here I thought we'd have a calm, pleasant dinner without any drama. Sorry, guys."

"Hey, it's not your fault," Bree said.

"I hope Quinn's okay," Billie said softly.

"Why wouldn't he be?" Will asked.

"I don't know. I have this suspicion he's chasing a lead when he shouldn't be. I can't think of any other reason he wouldn't be around."

A sudden knock sent her flying toward the door, but Will blocked her. "Absolutely not. Step back." He eyed the peephole, glanced at Billie and flung open the door.

Aiden stormed into the room. "I got your page and came right down. What happened?"

"A threatening note in the gift basket," Bree blurted out.

Billie's heart sank that it wasn't Quinn.

"Where's the note?" Aiden asked.

Billie pointed to the credenza. Aiden read the note and frowned. "No one ate anything out of this basket?"

"No," Billie said.

"Almost," Bree added.

He snapped his attention to his sister. "But you're okay."

"Thanks to Billie knocking it out of my hand."

"Will called the detective," Billie said. "Aiden, where's Quinn?"

"The P.I. found a lead and they headed into the mountains a few hours ago."

"Without telling me?" Billie said.

"You were resting."

Will glanced at his phone. "I've gotta get home for the girls." He glanced at Billie. "I can get a sitter and come back—"

"No," she said. "You need to be with your family. I'll be fine."

He gave her a quick hug and left.

Billie redirected her attention to Aiden. "Why did they head into the mountains?"

"They're checking something out."

"What?"

"I don't have the details."

"What aren't you telling me?" Billie pushed.

"You're wearing your sour-lemon face, big brother," Bree said. "You're definitely hiding something."

"I didn't like the idea of Quinn heading into the mountains with an inexperienced hiker. I wanted to join them, but I had to resolve an issue in the kitchen and they couldn't wait."

"Why are you so concerned?" Billie said.

"Because they're heading to a remote spot where they hope to find a cabin full of stolen property."

"But why would—" Billie's question was cut off by the simultaneous buzz of vibrating phones, which could only mean a search-and-rescue text had been sent.

Billie hadn't been field qualified so she didn't get the text messages, but would still get a call from Aiden to help in the command center at the trailhead for experience.

Bree gasped and looked at Aiden. "Is it…?

"It's Quinn."

A crack reverberated across the mountains and Quinn ducked, still shocked that they'd been shot at in a national park. It's not as if he and Cody had found the supposed cabin they were looking for, and no one but Aiden knew where they were headed.

Which meant someone had Quinn under surveillance.

Thankful that he'd managed to get cell service, Quinn studied his friend, who was crouched against a tree root growing out of the mountain wall. Quinn wondered if Cody was having a post-traumatic moment.

"I got through to 9-1-1," Quinn said, peeking around the corner. The gunfire had stopped, which was a good sign. "They'll send someone. It'll be fine."

"Uh, you sure about that?" Cody turned slightly and Quinn saw blood seeping through his friend's fingers as he gripped his shoulder.

"You're hit?" Quinn scrambled to him to assess the wound. All he could see was blood. Lots of it. Quinn ripped off his jacket, took off one of his shirts and shoved it against the wound. "Pressure, man, lots of pressure."

"Yeah, yeah. I know the drill." With a grunt, Cody held the material in place. "I guess this was a bad idea. We didn't even find the cabin."

"But we must be close or else why shoot at us?"

"Because they don't want us messing in their business?"

"I wish I knew who *they* were," Quinn said.

"I'll work on the Marshall Scrap Yard connection when we—"

"Let's get that bullet out of your shoulder first."

"You guys still there?" a man's voice called out.

Quinn glanced at Cody. "Answer him, keep him talking and I'll make my way around back."

"Quinn, don't. Wait for the rescue team."

"They won't send search and rescue until they know the area is secure, which means they'll send cops, but no medics." He eyed Cody's shoulder. "We can't wait that long."

"Hello, hello?" the voice taunted.

Quinn grabbed rope from his backpack and took off up the trail.

"We're here!" Cody shouted.

"You want to stay alive?"

"Yes, sir, we do."

"Then I've got an offer for you."

Quinn had worn camouflage colors today, so it would be unlikely the shooter would spot him. Quinn made it to the next plateau and dodged behind a tree for cover. He peered around the tree and spotted their assailant, leaning casually against a rock clutching a gun.

"What's the offer?" Cody said. Quinn could tell his voice was growing weaker.

Quinn narrowed his eyes and saw a pebbled trail leading to a concealed spot above the shooter. He headed in that direction, focused on neutralizing the shooter and getting Cody to the hospital.

"I need you to stay out of my business!" the guy ordered.

"Not a problem!"

"Seems to be a big problem."

Quinn sucked in air and ran as fast as he could, wishing he had a weapon.

"Then tell me what your business is and I'll make sure to stay away from it," Cody said.

Almost there. Looked like about 200 meters. He could do it. He could get there before—

Another shot rang out and Quinn hit the dirt.

"What was that for?" Cody called out.

"Making sure you took me seriously."

"I've already been hit. I get that you're serious."

Quinn scrambled to his feet and kept running.

"What about your friend?" the guy said.

"What about him?"

"Does he take me seriously?"

Great, if Quinn didn't answer, the guy might get suspicious and if he did answer he'd know Quinn's position.

"He's unconscious," Cody bluffed.

"He's dead?"

"Not yet, but he will be if we don't get help."

Quinn stopped short and peered down below. The shooter was pacing, as if he'd suddenly grown a conscience and was worried about what he'd done.

Quinn dodged out of sight. Took a deep breath. Got to his feet. He texted Cody, directing him to distract the guy.

"You must feel like a big man shooting at defenseless hikers," Cody taunted.

"You're not defenseless," the guy answered.

Quinn tied the rope around a tree branch and waited for the shooter to start talking again.

"You're working for Bronson's wife."

Quinn secured the rope around his waist and got ready to rappel.

"What do you want with her, anyway?" Cody asked. "She didn't do anything to you."

"Her husband cheated us, he—"

Quinn jumped, landed behind the shooter and tackled him to the ground. His gun went flying over the edge. Quinn got hold of the guy's neck and squeezed. The shooter elbowed Quinn in the ribs, once, twice, but Quinn didn't let go.

The guy got to his feet and slammed Quinn against the mountain wall. Air rushed from Quinn's lungs and his grip loosened. The shooter used the advantage to deliver another elbow to Quinn's ribs. The pain was starting to get to him. It wouldn't have been so bad had Quinn not been kicked in the chest last night. Quinn struggled to hold on, but the man broke free and violently shoved Quinn aside.

Stumbling to the edge of the trail, Quinn gripped the rope and steadied himself, watching the guy sprint away. He probably figured he was at a disadvantage without his gun.

Quinn bent over and took a few shallow breaths, trying to regain his equilibrium. "Cody, he's gone!" he shouted.

Silence. Quinn untied the rope and headed back to his friend. He whipped out his phone and called Aiden.

"Quinn, where are you?" Aiden answered.

Quinn gave him coordinates. "Cody's been shot. We need someone with medical training."

"Sheriff's office won't let us up there because of the gunfire."

"I disarmed the shooter and he took off. It's safe to retrieve us. Get up here, fast! Cody's unconscious."

The SAR team must have sprinted the mile and a half uphill to get to them so quickly, Quinn thought, as they led a medic to the scene. Once the bleeding stopped, they strapped Cody into the litter and started down.

Quinn continued to scan the area for any sign of the shooter, but the guy was long gone. Although Quinn kicked himself for not being able to detain him for police, he was more concerned about Cody.

As they approached the command center at the trailhead, Quinn spotted two police cars and an ambulance.

Then he saw Billie, her long brown hair framing her worried face, her hands firmly planted on her hips. From her posture, he guessed he was in for a lecture.

"I'll see you at the hospital," he said to Cody, who was drifting in and out of consciousness.

As the SAR team handed Cody off to the EMTs, Aiden and Billie approached Quinn.

"You okay?" Aiden asked.

"Yeah, I'm fine." He risked a glance at Billie.

Her furious expression melted into relief. Without warning, she wrapped her arms around his waist and squeezed tight. "I was so worried."

Her breath against his neck warmed him from the inside out.

"I'm tough." He broke the embrace. "You know that."

"Yeah, we'll see how tough you are when your brother gets here."

"You didn't," he said.

"Ah, so now I've got your attention." She led him away from the group and gripped his arm. "How could you put yourself at risk like that?"

"We had no idea someone was going to use us as target practice."

"Always with the jokes." She started to walk away.

"Billie—" he gently grabbed her arm "—it's okay. I'm fine. Cody will be fine."

She shook her head, wouldn't look at him.

"Or is there something else?"

"I got a gift basket with a threatening note."

"And I almost ate the chocolate," Bree said.

"The cops have collected it for testing," Aiden said.

Quinn studied Billie's defeated expression. "Aw, honey, I'm sorry." Now it was his turn to pull her close for a hug.

Aiden and Bree walked away, respecting Quinn's need for a private moment with Billie.

"I'm so sorry I wasn't there." Quinn rocked slightly, hoping the motion would soothe her. "Maybe you should reconsider leaving town."

"Absolutely not. I'm more determined than ever to figure out who these guys are, and I have an idea where to look. I was checking email and got a renewal notice on Rick and my family email address for a storage unit."

"How does that help us?"

"I didn't know we had a storage unit."

"Interesting."

"We could go check it out—"

."How about we go tomorrow? I could use one calm, un-eventful evening."

"Oh right, of course. You're probably exhausted." She glanced down. "I'm sorry for being so insensitive."

He tipped her chin with his forefinger so she'd look into his eyes. "No need to apologize. Let's go home."

The next morning Billie rose early and was ready to go by seven. As she gazed out her window onto the beautiful grounds, she remembered Quinn's comment last night, *let's go home,* and smiled to herself. Somehow the slip felt right; it felt normal. But when they got to the resort they went their separate ways. Quinn retreated into his apartment and Billie went to her suite where she had dinner with Bree and discussed the day's events.

Bree could tell Billie was still thinking about Quinn and challenged her to call him if she were worried. Billie sensed Quinn needed space to come down from the adrenaline rush of his afternoon. He could also use a little help from God to get his balance, but she wouldn't push it. When the time was right she'd make the suggestion.

She'd said her morning prayers, read a Bible passage and was waiting for Quinn. Something fluttered in her belly at the thought of spending the morning with him, or maybe even the entire day.

What are you thinking about, girl? This isn't a date.

As she studied the grounds, Bree came into view and waved. Billie smiled and returned the gesture.

Someone knocked at the door. She went and spied through the peephole. Quinn. With a quick breath, she swung open the door.

"You ready?" he asked.

"Sure," she said, turning to get her purse, but not before she'd noticed how handsome he looked today in black jeans and a knit shirt that showed off his broad shoulders.

"Did you get breakfast?"

"Yep." She grabbed her purse and turned.

"French toast with whipped cream and pecans?"

"How did you know?"

He smiled and her insides lit up. Oh boy, it was going to be a long day.

"What?" he questioned.

"I'm sorry?" She headed into the hallway and he followed.

"That look."

"Who knows, my brain is all over the place."

"I know the feeling." Quinn led her to a back entrance where a car was waiting.

"Joe's back?" she said.

"He is."

Quinn opened the car door. She climbed inside and greeted Joe. "So we didn't scare you off yesterday?"

"No, ma'am. Takes a lot to scare me off."

Quinn got into the backseat and they left.

"How's Cody?" she asked.

"He's okay, but out of commission for a while." Quinn shook his head. "I should have seen that coming."

"They're after me, not you, Quinn. How could you know?"

Quinn shrugged and glanced out the window.

"At least you got a look at your attacker."

"Not a good one. Although I felt his beard and saw a birthmark on the side of his neck."

"A beard, so it's the same guy who assaulted me?"

"Could be. I wish I'd been able to detain him."

"Hey." She touched his arm. "You saved Cody's life and your own. That's what's important."

"Yeah, well, I should anticipate this stuff before it blows up in our faces. I keep getting blindsided."

Her hand drifted down his arm to his hand, resting beside him on the seat. Studying his reaction, she threaded her fingers through his. Without looking at her, he curled his fingers, holding on to her. Silence filled the car. Not an awkward silence, but a contemplative, peaceful silence.

"Need some music?" Joe offered.

"No, I'm good," Billie said.

Twenty minutes later they arrived at the storage facility. Quinn directed Joe to keep watch outside, while he and Billie went to the office. She paid the bill and explained that her husband had died and she didn't know where he'd left the key. After showing her ID, the clerk unlocked the unit and went to the office.

"Ready?" Quinn said, gripping the door handle.

"No, but go for it."

He shoved the sliding door open to reveal a twelve-foot square unit packed with boxes and small pieces of antique furniture. She tentatively went inside.

"You recognize any of this?" Quinn said.

"Nope."

She wandered to a plastic bin and cracked open the top. Gold jewelry sparkling with gemstones shone back at her.

"Oh boy."

Quinn peeked over her shoulder. "You've got expensive taste," he teased.

"Funny. Who do you think it belongs to?" she asked, feeling bad that people were missing their precious keepsakes because of Rick.

"The police can figure that out." He led her to a small table and pointed to a schematic drawing of what looked like a house. "Does this look familiar?"

She considered the drawing, trying to figure out where she'd seen it before.

The sound of the rolling door grated against her nerve endings.

The door slammed shut and she gasped. "Quinn!"

He protectively shifted her behind him.

The lights went out, plunging them into complete darkness.

EIGHT

Quinn pulled Billie against his chest. "Shh, it's okay."

Fighting the self-condemnation at not anticipating this turn of events, he used the flashlight app on his smartphone to do a 360 scan of the storage area.

"There." He pointed with the flashlight. "Get behind those boxes."

"What are you going to do?" Billie clung tighter.

"I'm getting us out of here."

"We could wait for Joe."

"Who knows if they got to him already. Go on." He led her to the corner, then scanned the area for a make-shift weapon. He spotted fireplace tools and grabbed a poker off the rack. "Here—" he handed the phone to Billie "—shine this toward the door. But once I open it, you stay out of sight, hear me?"

"I should have a poker, too."

"You won't need one."

"Just in case."

He couldn't fault her for wanting to be prepared, although Quinn wasn't going to let anyone close enough to physically harm her. He snatched another tool off the fireplace rack— a shovel—and handed it to her.

"Stay back," he said.

She nodded.

"Okay, point the phone at the door."

She did as ordered and he gripped the handle with one hand while clenching the poker with the other.

Quinn took a deep breath and tried the door. It wasn't locked. He flung it open, making a wide arc in front of him with the poker. There was no one there. Light from the hallway spilled into the storage unit.

"Is he gone?" Billie stepped out from behind the boxes.

"Looks like it." He motioned to her with his hand and shifted her behind him. An outside door closed with a crash.

"Think he left?" she whispered.

"Can't assume anything."

As they headed for the exit, the sound of footsteps echoed from around the corner.

Quinn pulled her into an alcove leading to the bathrooms. Adrenaline pumped through his body. Joe had to have seen the guy enter the building, right? Billie clenched the material of his shirt into a ball. In that moment, Quinn realized how much he wanted to protect her.

He unclenched her fingers and mouthed the word *stay*. She shook her head, and he framed her cheek with his hand, leaned forward and brushed her lips with a brief kiss. It was impulsive and probably insane, yet it made complete sense to Quinn in that moment.

Leaning forward, he whispered in her ear. "I'll be right back."

He turned and took off toward the sound, glad he'd worn quiet-soled gym shoes today.

He appreciated Billie's trusting expression just now after he'd kissed her and whispered in her ear. It was that image that was driving him forward, straight into another dangerous confrontation. But he'd do whatever was necessary to keep her safe.

He turned the corner, flung open the door and spotted a guy running across the gravel parking lot. Clenching his poker, Quinn took off, vaguely registering that their SUV was empty.

The guy sprinted toward a black sedan and whipped the door open.

Quinn sprinted toward the car, swinging the poker. He wouldn't let the guy escape. The guy slammed his door shut just as Quinn made contact with the poker. He whacked the driver's-side window, splintering the glass, then went after the front tire to disable the car. At least the guy wouldn't get far.

Quinn heard the side door open and he darted over the hood of the car, yanked the guy out by his jacket collar and shoved him to the ground. The guy landed on his stomach. Quinn pressed his knee into the guy's lower back and yanked his wrists behind him. "What do you want?"

"Get off of me."

Quinn noticed the birthmark on the side of his neck. This was the same guy who shot Cody, maybe the same guy who assaulted Billie.

"Man, you are looking at serious jail time," Quinn said.

"If I were you, I'd be more worried about your girlfriend than my future."

Quinn flipped the guy over. "Who else is with you?"

The guy cracked a sinister smile.

"Answer me!" Quinn pulled him to his feet and slugged him in the gut.

"Quinn Donovan!"

Quinn glanced to his right and spotted Detective Issacs heading his way. Another squad car, lights flashing, roared into the parking lot.

Quinn dragged the assailant toward the detective. "Here, I've got to check on Billie." Quinn took off, but called over his shoulder. "That's the guy who shot Cody Monroe!"

He rushed to the storage facility door, but it was locked. It must automatically lock when customers leave. He pounded on the door and called Billie's name, but she probably couldn't hear him.

The facility manager came out of his office to speak with the cops. Quinn went to him, "I need to get in."

"Who are you?" a patrolman asked, approaching him.

"Quinn Donovan. My friend is inside. There could be another guy, his partner." He motioned to the shooter Issacs was handcuffing.

"He's with us!" Issacs called across the parking lot.

The cop nodded to the storage facility manager and he unlocked the door.

"Sir, you should—" the cop said, but Quinn was already gone.

He bolted down the long aisle. "Billie!"

Nothing.

"No, no, no," he muttered. There wasn't a back exit as far as he could tell so she still had to be here.

He raced up one aisle and down the other, turning the corner to the alcove where he'd left her. "Billie!" he cried.

"Quinn?" a soft voice responded.

The door to the women's restroom swung open. With a cautious expression she stepped out.

He pulled her against his chest. "You're okay, you're okay," he whispered more to convince himself to breathe normally, than to comfort Billie.

"I thought I heard something so I ducked into the bathroom. I figured even a criminal would avoid going into the ladies' room."

"Donovan!" the detective called out.

"Back here!" Quinn led Billie out of the bathroom.

Detective Issacs rushed over to them. "Is she okay?"

"Yeah, just frightened," Quinn said.

"Detective, how did you get here so fast?" Billie asked.

"We've been keeping an eye on you two. It seems like wherever you go, these guys are sure to follow." He eyed

Billie. "We've got the shooter cuffed in the backseat of a squad car, which is good considering I might have had to arrest your knight in shining armor here after a few more minutes of interrogation."

"Quinn?" Billie said. "What did you—"

"He implied he had an accomplice. I think he was just trying to throw me off by hinting Billie was still in danger."

Detective Issacs glanced from Billie to Quinn. "Ah, now I understand the desperation of your interrogation techniques."

Wanting to change the subject, Quinn motioned around the corner. "We found a storage unit with what I'm guessing are stolen goods."

"Let's check it out," Issacs said.

As Quinn led him to the unit, he kept Billie close with a steady arm around her shoulders. More than anything in the world he wanted her to feel safe. They turned the corner to the unit and Issacs peeked inside.

"Someone was busy," he said scanning the property, then glanced at Billie. "How did you find this place?"

"I received an email to renew our contract. I didn't know we had a storage unit. Obviously none of this is mine."

"You didn't call me when you decided to come here because…?"

Quinn didn't immediately answer. He couldn't. His body was still coming down from the surge of adrenaline pulsing through his veins. When he'd called out Billie's name and she hadn't answered he'd felt gutted, completely lost.

He was supposed to be protecting her, yet danger kept finding them. Or was it Quinn's bad judgment that made him walk her directly into the line of fire?

"We didn't want to bother you," Billie offered. "Checking out a storage unit shouldn't have been dangerous. Besides, won't we get to the bottom of this quicker if we follow different leads?"

"Spoken like a detective wannabe," Issacs said.

"What I want is to put an end to this case so I don't feel threatened all the time," Billie said.

"I get it—I do," Issacs said. "But you two have to stop playing detective and let me do my job."

"Of course," Billie said.

Detective Issacs analyzed the goods. "I'll call forensics." He motioned them out and pulled the door closed. "Good news is we have the perp who shot Cody Monroe. Mrs. Bronson, I'd like you to take a look at him and see if he's also the one who assaulted you on the trail the other day."

They left the building and Issacs escorted them to a squad car. Billie was a good ten feet away when she stopped short and gripped Quinn's arm. "It's him."

"You sure?" Issacs said. "You want to get a closer look?"

"I'm as close as I ever want to get to that guy again. I'm positive."

"I'll take him in for questioning," Issacs said. "I want the two of you to go home and not think about this case. You read me?" He looked directly at Quinn.

"Yes, sir," Quinn answered. Quinn would appreciate the opportunity to decompress, maybe take care of a little business. He glanced at their SUV. "I wonder what happened to Joe?"

"He's missing?" Issacs asked.

"He brought us here, but I don't see him—"

Joe stumbled around the SUV clutching his head.

"Hey, you okay?" Quinn asked as they approached.

"Embarrassed, but fine. I heard something and went to investigate. He got me good," he said, rubbing his head.

"The perp's in the squad car. You need me to call an EMT?" the detective offered.

Joe waved him off. "Nah, I'm good."

"Okay, well—" he glanced at Quinn "—remember what I said."

* * *

Saying they'd had enough excitement for one day, Quinn suggested they take it easy and relax. Billie figured he was motivated by the need to get some work done; after all, he'd been taking care of her 24/7 since her fall.

As the hours stretched into the afternoon, she realized her work wasn't over. She should continue going through family files and documents she'd abandoned after Rick's death. If he'd lied to her about renting a storage unit, what other secrets were out there waiting to go off like ticking bombs?

She'd asked Aiden to swing by her apartment, get the lockbox she kept in her closet and bring it to her. She wasn't sure what she expected to find in the piles now strewn across her bed, but she'd hoped to uncover a clue that could help Detective Issacs.

A knock sounded at her door. She padded across the room and looked through the peephole. Quinn smiled at her. She swung open the door.

"Thought I'd bring dinner," he said, wheeling a tray into her room.

"It's that late?" She followed him to the table beside the window.

"It's only five but I figured you'd be hungry." He glanced at her bed. "What's all this?"

"Family files, documents, stuff like that."

Quinn paused and glanced over his shoulder. "How did you—"

"Aiden got them for me."

"Oh," he said, glancing away, but not before a hint of disappointment flashed in his blue eyes.

"I asked him to pick up the box because I figured you were busy with work," she said.

"You don't have to explain."

"For some reason I feel like I do."

He placed the covered plates on the table and moved the cart aside.

She touched his arm. "Quinn?"

"Chef's special tonight is cedar planked salmon."

"Talk to me."

"About?"

"That look you just gave me."

"You must have imagined it."

"I was your personal assistant for nearly six months. I learned to read your expressions and your moods."

"Yeah, aren't you glad that gig is over?"

"Don't change the subject.

"I don't know what you want me to say."

"Tell me what you thought when I said Aiden picked up my documents."

He fiddled with the salt and pepper shakers. She placed her hand over his. "What flashed through your head?"

"That you didn't want to risk me screwing up again."

"Screwing up?"

"Issacs was right. They find us every time we head out, and yet I walked us directly into trouble, again."

"You couldn't have known he'd find us at the storage unit."

"I should have." He pinned her with intense and angry blue eyes.

But he wasn't angry with her.

"I should have assumed we were being watched. This whole thing started with some guy following you into the mountains. They followed us here from the hospital, followed us to the storage unit and threatened your life."

"None of which is your fault."

"Sure it is if I'm dumb enough to walk straight into the threat."

"Don't talk like that. You are anything but dumb."

"Some people might disagree."

She motioned for him to sit down. "I dare you to find me one person who thinks you're dumb."

"You've never met my stepmother." He collapsed in the chair, lifted the cover off his plate and quickly replaced it.

"What's wrong?"

"Lost my appetite." He glanced out the window.

"Tell me about her."

He snapped his attention to Billie. "Why?"

"It might help."

"What, understand me better? You know me better than my own brother. Trust me, you know enough."

"No, it might help to loosen all this angst twisting your stomach into knots."

"What makes you think my stomach's twisted into knots?"

"Just a guess." She removed her cover and inhaled the delicious scent of salmon, rice and baked broccoli. "How old were you when your mother died?"

He lifted his cover and placed it on the table. "Ten."

Sadness caught in her throat at the image of a little Quinn standing beside his mother's coffin. She wanted to go to him, hug him, do something to ease the flatness of his voice. She knew if she showed any kind of emotion he'd shut down, and Quinn Donovan needed to get this story out.

"I'm sorry," she said, forking her salmon. "That must have been horrible."

"Yeah, well, Sophia came into the picture when I was eleven and my brother Alex was sixteen. He was a jock so he wasn't around much, then he enlisted in the army right out of high school. Dad worked overtime a lot, leaving me alone with her. I just wanted my mom back, ya know?" He forked his rice, but didn't eat. "I think Sophia resented having to raise a teenager. I acted out, trying to get Dad's attention, someone's attention. She'd get so mad at me." He shook his head.

"She didn't—"

"No, she never got physical. But sometimes the other stuff can leave deeper scars."

"Other stuff, you mean...?"

"She'd say stuff. She basically convinced me I drove my mother into an early grave."

Billie slammed her fork down. "How could she do that to a grieving little boy?"

Quinn shrugged. "She's a classic narcissist. I don't think Dad knew what he was getting into until it was too late."

"So he worked overtime to stay away from her?"

"At first he worked a lot to buy her things. Then as the years wore on, yeah, I guess he was staying away."

"Didn't he ask how you were doing?"

"He thought she was taking care of the emotional stuff. I mean, he was totally bamboozled by the woman at first, and by the time he figured out what she was, well, he was ashamed. I think he felt like he'd failed me. He could hardly look me in the eye."

Quinn suddenly looked at Billie. "Why am I telling you this?"

"Because it feels good to get it out."

"I guess." With a sad smile, he glanced at his food.

"What happened to her?" Billie asked.

"They eventually divorced. Dad got cancer and she didn't want to be his caregiver. She managed to empty his bank accounts before she skipped town."

"Did you report her to the police?"

"We didn't know until it was too late. Dad was too ashamed to pursue legal action. The damage was done."

His words rang heavy in the room. She'd obviously done worse damage than emptying a bank account.

"But she's out of your life now, so you don't have to think about her anymore, right?"

"Easier said than done, especially when you've left a path of destruction in your wake."

"What do you mean?"

"My marriage. Probably shouldn't have gotten married in the first place, but I wanted to prove I was lovable. Then I managed to destroy that because I wouldn't—" he glanced at Billie "—open up to her. There was this part of me I could never share. I was afraid she'd skewer me like Sophia did my dad."

"So, you still hear your stepmother's negative comments?"

"Oh, yeah."

"But you know they're all lies."

"Sometimes that's not enough."

"Sometimes a little divine intervention could help."

"Thanks for the suggestion, but guys like me aren't allowed to lean on guys like God."

"Don't say that. God loves all his children."

Quinn shook his head, signaling that part of the conversation was over, but Billie wasn't done.

"Quinn, will you do one thing for me?"

He glanced up with such vulnerability in his eyes.

"Will you relinquish your angst and emotional pain to God? Surrender it, and let him do the rest?"

He shrugged. She took his hand and bowed her head. "Dear Lord, please help Quinn find his way to peace by surrendering his pain, by letting go of his anger and by finding grace through Your love. Amen."

She opened her eyes and caught Quinn studying her as if he'd never seen her before. When she started to pull her hand away, he squeezed it and said, "Thank you."

She couldn't look away, couldn't break eye contact with this man who she'd always suspected had many layers protecting his heart. And now she understood why.

The phone rang, jarring them out of the moment. She

cleared her throat and reached behind her to answer. "Hello?"

"Mrs. Bronson?"

"Yes?"

"This is Detective Issacs. I wanted you to know that I'm getting some good information from the guy we arrested at the storage facility. Apparently he was sent to get in contact with you about your husband's involvement in a crime ring. Haven't figure out why yet, but with his help I'm confident we'll track down the leader of the group."

"What was my husband's role?"

"Transportation. He'd find various places to stash the items throughout the Northwest."

"I see."

"The suspect said something else." He hesitated.

"What?"

"A year ago when you and your husband were rescued by search and rescue?"

"Yes?"

"Your husband had been ordered to kill you."

NINE

"Oh," Billie said, completely stunned.

"They thought you'd discovered what he was doing and feared you'd contact the authorities. They told your husband to make it look like a hiking accident."

All Billie could think about was how she'd tended to Rick, prayed with him during those last hours before SAR medical personnel arrived.

Yet he'd been planning to kill her?

"Mrs. Bronson?" the detective said.

"Yes, I'm here."

"Why would they think you had something on them?"

"I have no idea. Why did they wait so long to come after me?"

"When you left town they lost track of you. They probably figured if you had damaging evidence you would have gone to the police."

"And now?"

"I'd be speculating, but I'm guessing you have something they need, maybe it's in your husband's things. I'll keep working on this guy for answers. He's got a lawyer, but wants to negotiate a deal so I've got some leverage. The good news is, it looks like the rest of them are out of state," he said. "So you should be relatively safe for now."

"Oh, okay, thanks."

"Still, it won't hurt to be cautious."

"Of course. Thanks for the call." She hung up and shook her head.

"What is it?" Quinn said.

"If anyone's dumb it's me."

"Was that—?"

"Detective Issacs. Apparently Rick took me out on a romantic hike to get me alone so he could…" she hesitated "…kill me."

"Aw, Billie, I'm so sorry." He reached over and touched her hand.

"I had no idea, not even an inkling. I thought he was making an effort, you know, trying to get our marriage on track. I am so naive."

"You're hopeful, that's not a bad thing."

He continued to stroke her hand. She couldn't handle it, couldn't handle the caring gesture from this guarded man. She thought she understood Rick and his desperation to provide for the woman he loved. Yet he'd planned to kill her?

"What happened that day you two went hiking?" Quinn asked.

She slipped her hand out from under his. "Rick packed lunches and said he wanted to get away for a few hours, explore nature. We headed into Snoqualmie National Forest. I took the lead so he could catch me in case I tripped, at least that's what he'd said." She remembered hiking in silence, breathing in the crisp air, and how the mountain chill cooled her skin as they worked up a sweat. "It started to rain and got slippery. We ducked beneath an overhang for shelter, decided to eat lunch and wait for the rain to ease up and then…" An odd scene replayed itself in her mind.

"Billie?" Quinn prompted.

She glanced at him. "I was about to drink lemonade and he knocked it out of my hand and lectured me about drinking lemonade when I should be drinking water. It was nonsensical. He grew agitated. We argued and he stormed out of the shelter, pacing frantically. I was scared, Quinn. I didn't know what had set him off. I mean, lemonade? Really?"

"Then what happened?"

"We argued. He lost his footing and fell fifty feet to the ledge below. I was…I was in shock for a minute. I couldn't believe it had happened. Then I lowered myself down there."

She'd blamed herself because if she hadn't set him off he wouldn't have left the shelter and fallen.

"He packed the lunches that day?" Quinn asked.

"Yes."

"But he yelled at you for drinking lemonade?"

She nodded.

"That makes no sense, Billie. Unless…"

"What?"

He glanced at her with compassion in his eyes. "Maybe he spiked the lemonade but at the last minute had a change of heart."

"Spiked it?"

"Sure, so you'd be loopy and fall to your death."

It all fell into place: her husband's loving behavior after months of being withdrawn; suggesting a romantic hike; then not letting her drink the lemonade.

"And here I thought he was trying to save our marriage," she muttered.

"You always look for the good in people."

"Which makes me naive and foolish."

"Don't say that." He reached for her hand again, but she stood and paced to the window, crossing her arms over her chest.

"He couldn't do it, Billie. Which means he still loved you."

She stared out the window at a family—Mom, Dad and four kids—playing volleyball on a sandpit bordered by gorgeous green grass. A family. She'd always hoped she'd have one of her own. But right now she doubted she could ever trust her heart to another man. Sure, she knew Rick was struggling, but he wasn't a killer. Was he?

"Sweetheart, don't do this to yourself," Quinn said coming up behind her and touching her shoulder.

"In the last year of our marriage Rick never called me sweetheart." She looked into his blue eyes. "Yet it sounds so natural coming from you." She read tenderness in his eyes, maybe even love.

His phone buzzed and he glanced at it. "It's an SAR text. I'll check in with Aiden." Quinn wandered to the other side of the room to make the call.

She snapped her attention from his broad shoulders. This was crazy, she was slipping again, falling into a false sense of security with a man she knew had no intention of committing to her or any other woman for that matter.

Although she understood why Quinn walled himself off to emotional connections with women, she couldn't offer her heart to a man who would surely break it due to his own emotional pain.

If only he'd surrender that albatross weighing down his heart. *Please, God, help Quinn.*

"I guess an Alzheimer's patient went for an unauthorized walk and hasn't been seen since lunch," Quinn said, eyeing his phone.

"Who is it?"

"A guy named Donald Vicars."

"I helped find him last month."

"They've got plenty of help."

"Where was he last seen?"

"By the Wallace Falls trailhead."

"I know where he's going, Quinn. We've got to help."

Quinn shook his head. "They've got a full team to handle it."

"A team of strangers. He'll be terrified. Donald knows

me. If a bunch of people corner him he could turn aggressive or take off deeper into the mountains."

"It's too dangerous."

"The bearded man is in custody and Detective Issacs made it sound like the others aren't in town. I won't let fear keep me from helping Donald."

"Billie—"

"It's almost seven. We have two maybe three hours of light to find him. Can I borrow a pack?"

"I'm not going to win this argument, am I?"

"Smart man. Let's go put together a pack while you call Aiden and tell the field leader I'm on my way."

Quinn had made it clear that he didn't like the idea of Billie going on a mission, even a short one with a team of four SAR members. She noticed that as he hiked alongside her, his eyes continued to roam the forest on either side of them, probably anticipating threats from all directions.

They didn't have much time to find Donald, and the setting sun would only make their jobs harder. Luckily, she knew exactly where to go.

"Why Wallace Falls?" he asked her.

"Actually it's not as far as the falls, but along the way there's a spot where he and his high school sweetheart used to sit by the river and have a picnic. It was their special place."

"And Donald remembers that?"

"It's easier for him to remember distant memories than recent ones."

"How did you keep him calm the last time you found him?"

"I kept him talking about the past, didn't argue with him and told the team to keep their voices down."

"You seem to know a lot about this condition," Quinn said.

"My grandfather had it. He lived with us as long as we

could take care of him, but it got to be an around-the-clock job so we found him a place where he'd be safe."

"We're losing daylight," one of the SAR team members commented.

"It's right around the next switchback." She stopped and looked at the team of four that accompanied her and Quinn. "I'll need you guys to stay back at first. Keep your voices down, don't ask questions or contradict him, okay?"

"Sure," the lead, Tyler Grayson, said.

Truth was, they probably didn't need four men and a woman to recover Donald, but these guys were passionate about search and rescue.

"If Donald calls you by name, roll with it," Billie said. "He has two sons who live out of state, but he might confuse you with them."

With a deep breath, she turned the corner and climbed off the trail toward the river. She spotted Donald on the ground and rushed to him, worry tangling her insides. "Donald?"

As she reached for his wrist to check his pulse, his eyes fluttered open.

"Vivienne?" he said.

"I'm glad I found you," she said.

"Is it time to go?"

She helped him sit up. "Yes, the sun is going down soon."

His eyes widened with worry. "Are we late?"

"No, we're fine, but we need to head home now."

Donald gazed at the bubbling river. "It's beautiful."

"Yes, it is." She encouraged him to stand.

Quinn reached out to help steady Donald and the older man jerked away, frightened.

"Donald, this is my friend, Quinn. He's a seasoned hiker and he'd like to lead us down."

"I'm a seasoned hiker," Donald shot back.

"That's right," she said. "Maybe you could teach Quinn a few things about hiking."

Donald's attitude changed completely. "The first thing to remember is always to be prepared with water and food." He reached behind him and realized he didn't have a pack. "Where's my pack? Someone stole it!"

"I carried it for you." Billie took off her pack and held it out for Donald to strap on his shoulders.

"Thank you," he said.

"You ready?" she said.

"Want me to lead?" Quinn offered.

"Yes, and I'll give you more tips as we go," Donald said.

"Donald, I brought a few friends with me and they're waiting around the corner."

"Why did you bring friends?"

"They wanted to meet you. They heard what an expert hiker you are."

Donald puffed up his chest.

Quinn helped Billie guide Donald back to the trail. Relief washed over her that they'd found him where she thought he'd be. Now they needed to get him to the trailhead where an ambulance was waiting. He didn't seem injured, but it was a good idea to have him checked out.

They approached the trail and the waiting team.

"Guys, this is Donald," Quinn introduced.

Donald nodded at the men. "You boys staying for dinner?"

The men looked at each other, but Tyler caught on. "We'd love to, sir. Shall we head back?"

"Lead the way." Donald motioned with his hand.

Two of the men led the group while Tyler followed close behind.

"It'll be nice to have a full table of guests, Vivienne," Donald said to Billie. "We're having…what are we having again?"

"Meatloaf and mashed potatoes," she offered.

"My favorite."

* * *

They made it down without incident and Billie asked Quinn to take her to the hospital to be with Donald until his family arrived. A few minutes later, Donald's two daughters, who lived locally, showed up and thanked Billie profusely. It felt empowering to be helpful as opposed to being a victim and hiding out. She held on to that feeling as she headed to the lobby to find Quinn.

"Billie?"

She turned and spotted Bree heading her way.

"What are you doing here?" Billie asked.

"Volunteer shift. Just got off," Bree said. "I heard about Donald. Is he okay?"

"Seems to be. The doctors are checking him out now."

Quinn wandered over to them and Billie offered a smile. "Thanks for bringing me. I think it helped keep him calm."

"You are amazing, you know that?" he said.

Bree's jaw dropped.

"What?" Quinn said.

"I guess I've never heard a man pay such a nice compliment to a woman, and in public."

"Then you're hanging out with the wrong men," Quinn teased.

"Yeah," Bree glanced away.

Billie sensed her friend getting hooked by her tumultuous past. Hoping to shake Bree out of it, Billie asked, "Since you're off, want to give me a ride to the resort?"

"Hey, what about me?" Quinn said.

"You've been wanting to visit Cody since he was admitted. This is the perfect opportunity." She touched Bree's shoulder. "Or did you have plans tonight?"

"Nope, no plans."

"Great, you can take me back and we can catch up."

"You'll go straight to your room?" Quinn said.

"You sound like her father," Bree teased, snapping out of her darkness.

"It's my job to protect her," Quinn countered.

"I thought she had a security guy," Bree said.

"He didn't come with us on the mission and we headed straight here after we found Donald." Billie turned to Quinn. "I'll see you at the resort?"

"Yes, ma'am."

Billie hesitated, then did what felt natural. She hugged him. She felt his arms press against her back and squeeze just enough to let her know he was there for her, and maybe even appreciated the hug. She broke the embrace and looked at Bree, who raised an eyebrow.

"We've been through a lot together," Billie explained, looped her arm through Bree's and headed out.

"No stops," Quinn said.

"Not a one." Billie whispered to her friend, "Let's order room service."

"Hot fudge sundaes?" Bree said with delight in her voice.

"With sprinkles and macadamia nuts."

"Potato chips?"

"Girlfriend, you are trouble."

They giggled as they rode the elevator down to the parking garage.

"So what's happening with the case?" Bree asked.

"They caught the bearded guy this morning. He followed us to a storage facility Rick had rented."

"And you knew nothing about it?"

"Nope."

"You and I must have been absent the day they handed out the textbook on men," Bree said.

"No kidding."

"What about Quinn?"

"What about him?"

Bree shrugged. "He seems like a ladies' man, dedicated

to work first and everything else second, yet the way he acts with you is incongruous with his reputation."

"*Incongruous,* yeah. That's a good word for it."

The elevator doors opened and they headed to Bree's SUV.

"It's a shame," Bree said.

"What?"

"Everything that happened with Rick has made you skittish, but it's pretty obvious that you and Quinn would make a great couple."

"He has no interest in committing to one woman."

"You sure about that?"

"About 95 percent sure, yeah. I lived in his coach house, remember? I saw the women he paraded in and out of his place."

"Maybe he hadn't found the right one. Think about it, you call him out on stuff, yet you're nurturing and compassionate, which he obviously needs. I think—"

Bree was cut off by the sound of screeching tires.

Lights temporarily blinded Billie as she sensed a car barreling toward them. She dove between two cars, and glanced over her shoulder.

Bree hadn't moved.

"Bree!" Billie rushed to her friend and knocked her out of the way as the car passed. They stumbled to the ground, Billie's heart hammering into her throat. "Are you okay?" she asked Bree, who nodded with confusion.

The squeal of the driver hitting the brakes pierced the air. Their attacker wasn't done.

TEN

"Keys," Billie demanded of Bree.

Bree glanced at her empty hand, then to the spot where they'd been standing. The keys sat in the middle of the garage, directly in the line of the driver's path.

Billie pulled out her phone and shoved it at Bree. "Call 9-1-1."

"No, wait."

Billie took off as a plan formulated in her head. The driver gunned the engine, but she realized he'd be driving backward, which gave her the advantage.

She ignored the roar of the threatening engine, rushed across the parking lot and snatched the keys.

She dashed toward a black car for cover, hitting the alarm button on Bree's key FOB. Her attacker sped backward, colliding with a car only a few feet from Billie. That collision set off another car alarm. She hoped the alarms would draw security's attention.

Billie weaved between cars to put distance between herself and the driver.

Suddenly an alarm blared overhead, red lights flashing.

Peeking out from between two cars, she saw taillights of the attack car speeding away. Billie rushed to her friend, who was being comforted by a hospital security guard. The alarm was so loud they couldn't talk to each other, so he motioned them to the elevators. He stuck his key in a console on the wall and turned off the alarm.

Bree was visibly shaking.

"It's okay. You're okay," Billie said, hugging her.

The elevator doors opened and Quinn rushed to them. "What happened?"

"Someone tried to run us down," Billie said. "But we're okay."

Quinn ran his hand through his hair, clearly agitated.

"Need to get checked out upstairs, Breanna?" the security guard asked.

"No," Bree snapped. "I want to go home."

"You can't drive in that condition," Quinn said. "I'll drive you both to the resort."

"But I can—"

"End of discussion," Quinn said.

He shook the security guard's hand. "Thanks."

"They should file a police report," the guard suggested.

"They will." Quinn motioned them to his car, but glanced over his shoulder at the guard. "Police will want to see video footage to help identify the driver. Expect Detective Issacs to stop by."

"Will do."

Quinn escorted them to his SUV and opened the back door for Bree. She climbed in and he shut the door.

Not looking at Billie, he opened the passenger door for her.

"Quinn?"

"Please get in the car."

"You're angry with me?"

"Not now."

His gaze drifted to the ground and Billie did as requested. Either he was upset with her for not waiting for him to give her a ride home or…

He was beating himself up, blaming himself for not being there to protect her. She should have known he'd go there, but she wasn't going to let him sink into that place of failure again.

* * *

Once they made it to the resort, Billie invited Bree to hang out in her room for a bit. Billie appreciated the company, plus it took her mind off what had nearly happened in the garage.

She'd been surprised when Quinn didn't argue with Billie about spending time alone with her friend. Billie expected him to muscle his way into her suite and suffer through girl talk in order to make sure she was safe.

Quinn still hadn't shared what he'd been stewing about during the silent car ride home. The minutes felt like hours as she tried to engage him in conversation, but he could only manage one-word answers. She'd confront him tomorrow, in private, because she didn't like it when he shut down, and shut her out.

"This tastes wonderful," Bree said, dipping her spoon into a sloppy chocolate sundae topped with pecans and multicolored sprinkles.

"You've earned it. Sorry that you got pulled into this mess." Billie spooned ice cream and tapped it on the lip of the glass dish. "They have the main guy in custody so we thought I was relatively safe."

"It's not your fault." Bree sighed. "I owe you an apology for making it worse."

"What do you mean?"

"The way I froze when the headlights hit me. I guess—" she hesitated and swirled her spoon in the softening ice cream "—I was having a flashback."

"About Thomas?" Billie asked. Bree had confided in Billie about her abusive ex-boyfriend.

Bree studied her ice cream as she spoke. "When he'd hit me, in that moment, I was always so shocked. I couldn't believe it was really happening, and I'd completely shut down. Later he'd be so charming and loving, that a part of me was convinced I'd imagined it. When I saw the headlights I thought, 'why would anyone be trying to run me down?' I couldn't wrap my head around it."

"They weren't aiming for you."

"That's not the point." She glanced at Billie. "Even after earning my black belt, I still feel so weak sometimes, and you're so strong. You saved my life, Billie."

"That's what friends are for, right? Now come on, let's eat these monstrosities before the ice cream melts."

Bree studied her. "You don't seem shaken by what happened tonight."

"I am. But I'm more frustrated and angry. We thought the man in custody was the only direct threat and now there's someone else? I don't get what they want from me. The bearded guy said he wanted to partner with me, and yet there have been multiple threats on my life. Why would they want me dead?"

"Because you know something?" Bree said.

"Doubtful. I hardly spoke to Rick during our last months together."

"You fought a lot, huh?"

"You can't fight if you're not even talking to each other." Billie shook her head. "It happened so slowly, then one day I woke up and it's like we weren't even speaking the same language. He stopped going to church, volunteering for Habitat for Humanity. We even dropped out of the dinner group we belonged to. He was isolating himself from everyone, even me." Billie shook her head. "Why am I talking about this?"

"Because you need to. Don't stop. It makes me feel good that I can help by listening."

"We drifted apart and there was nothing I could do to fix it." Billie glanced at Bree. "But there should have been, I was his wife for seven years. If he loved me, that love should have seen us through."

"Sometimes we do things for love that lead us in the wrong direction."

"Like you staying with Thomas?"

"And Rick wanting to provide for you, even if that meant doing something criminal."

Billie's cell rang and she recognized Will's phone number.

"Who is it?" Bree said, stirring the sprinkles around in her sundae.

"Will."

Bree raised a teasing eyebrow, as Billie took the call.

"Hi, Will."

"I heard what happened at the hospital. You okay?"

"Yes, I'm fine. No one was hurt."

"I thought you had Quinn Donovan and his twenty-four-hour security team with you at all times."

"They usually are, but Quinn was visiting a friend in the hospital."

"He should have known better. I wouldn't have left your side."

"Thanks, I appreciate that."

Someone knocked on the door. Bree crossed the room, eyed the peephole and swung open the door. Quinn wandered in.

"I know it's late, but I thought I might swing by," Will offered.

"Actually, I'm pretty wiped out. But thanks."

"Okay, well, call if you need anything."

"Thanks. Good night." Billie ended the call and turned to Quinn.

"Hey," she said.

He glanced across the room at the sundaes. He hadn't made eye contact since the incident in the garage.

"How's the ice cream?" he asked.

"Quite tasty, but not nearly enough sprinkles," Bree said.

"I'll notify the chef," Quinn joked.

"You're here awfully late," Billie said, glancing at the clock. It read 10:15 p.m.

"Sorry, guess I should have called. I wanted to see for myself that you ladies had everything you needed."

"I'm good," Bree said.

Billie stepped directly into Quinn's line of vision. He still wouldn't look at her. "I could use something," Billie said.

Quinn finally glanced at her, but only briefly.

"I want answers," Billie said. "Like who is still after me, who tried to run us down and, most important, why won't you look at me?"

Bree slowly put her spoon in the dish.

"They have a video image of the driver from the hospital and are sending it to local police departments for identification," Quinn said. "That should help them narrow down the suspect list."

"And you won't look at me because…?"

"You're imagining things."

"Look me in the eye and say that."

Quinn planted his hands on his hips and studied the floor.

"I forgot to call Mom and tell her I'm okay." Bree hurried into the bedroom and shut the door to give them privacy.

Billie studied Quinn, noting the narrowing of his eyes and tightness of his lips. "Quinn?"

"I can't do this right now."

"Well, I need to do this right now. What's bugging you?"

He snapped his attention to her, his blue eyes aflame with anger. "Let's see, the fact I shouldn't have let you leave this room for the SAR mission and I shouldn't have left your side at the hospital because the thought of…" He shook his head.

"What?" She squeezed his upper arm.

"The thought of you being hit by a car because I wasn't there is tearing me apart."

"What would you have done? Do you have superhero

powers I don't know about? Would you have stopped the car with your bare hands?"

He gently gripped her shoulders and looked deep into her eyes. "I could have protected you. But I didn't because I wasn't there."

"Quinn, I'm a big girl and eventually I'll have to learn to function without my knight in shining armor at my side."

"I know, I know," Quinn whispered. "But…I'm supposed to protect you."

"And you have so many times. Look, we all thought the threat was in custody. You couldn't have known."

"But—"

"I'm a strong and determined woman, Quinn. I don't need anyone taking care of me."

He released her shoulders and went to the window overlooking the grounds. Worried she might have offended him, she said, "I appreciate your commitment to my safety. We make a great team."

When he didn't respond, she stepped in front of him and smiled. "Hey, you." She touched his cheek and his jaw clenched as he continued to stare outside. "I mean it," she said. "It makes me anxious when you won't look at me. I feel like I've done something wrong."

He snapped his attention to her. "Don't try to take responsibility for my incompetence."

He was falling into a pool of self-condemnation and she had to somehow yank him out. "You need ice cream. Come on, I'll share."

Determined to change his dark mood, Billie went to the dining table and grabbed her dish. "I don't share my ice cream with just anyone," she started, "but I'll make an exception for the guy who's assigned himself my protector." She scooped vanilla ice cream onto a spoon and held it to his lips.

He narrowed his eyes at her. "I know what you're doing."

"Yeah, what's that?"

"You're trying to distract me."

"Is it working?"

"No." He hesitated and cracked a slight smile. "Yes."

"Score one for ice cream."

Instead of letting her spoon-feed him, he took the utensil from her hand. "I'm a big boy."

A big boy with a big heart. She felt a knowing smile play at her lips. No matter how guarded and confident Quinn appeared to the rest of the world, Billie saw the wounded man struggling to find peace.

The bedroom door cracked open. "Is it safe?" Bree said.

"Come on out," Billie said. "Quinn is about to finish off my sundae."

Bree joined them in the living room. "There's nothing like ice cream to make everything look better."

"You're right about that," Quinn said, studying Billie.

"So, what's on the agenda for tomorrow?" Bree asked.

"I'm diving headlong into boxes of stuff I put in storage after Rick's accident," Billie said. "There's got to be something in there that can help the police."

"But you're staying here, in your room, right?" Quinn confirmed.

"That's the plan."

"I'll get up early and get some work done, then I'll come down and help you sift through the boxes," Quinn said, placing his spoon on the food tray.

"Sounds good," Billie said.

"All right, I'd better go. I've got...I've got something to take care of." Quinn glanced around the room as if he was forgetting something. "Good, okay, well good night."

But instead of heading for the door, he took a few steps toward Billie and pulled her into a hug. She felt him inhale a long breath. He whispered into her ear, "Sweet dreams." He broke the hug and went to the door. "Good night, Breanna."

"Good night."

The door clicked shut behind him. With a raised eyebrow, Bree said, "What was that?"

"What, the hug? You've seen people hug before."

"Not like that I haven't."

The next morning Billie woke up sore all over from shoving Bree out of the way and slamming into a nearby car. Or was it the emotional turmoil that seemed to sap her energy today, the not knowing who was after her and from where the next threat would come?

Feeling more than a little tired, she ordered fruit, eggs and bacon for breakfast, hoping the protein would bring her around. An hour later she'd organized all her files and documents, ready to analyze every word and punctuation mark in the hopes of finding out why Rick's associates were after her.

She discovered paperwork she'd never seen before: a topographic map with a few spots circled in red, and a legal description of land she wasn't familiar with.

The suite phone rang and she grabbed it, hoping it was Quinn. "Hello?"

Silence answered her.

"Hello?" she tried again.

No one responded so she hung up. She didn't think anything of it and refocused on the topo map. Then a thought struck her: What if someone was calling to see if she was in the room? No, she was being paranoid.

But Billie had learned to respect and trust her gut instinct. She opened the door to her room. Joe, the day security guard, sat in a chair reading the morning paper.

"Good morning, ma'am. Everything okay?"

"It's probably nothing, but I had a crank call and—"

He abruptly stood and motioned her out of the room. "Let's go."

"But—"

"It's better to be cautious about these things."

"Where are we going?" she asked as they motored down the hall.

"Mr. Donovan said to take you to his apartment if I thought your suite had been compromised."

Joe kept looking over his shoulder as he escorted her down the hall.

"Shouldn't we call him first?"

"No, ma'am." He didn't even knock when they got to Quinn's apartment. He swiped a keycard and unlocked the door. Motioning her inside, Joe scanned the hallway and shut the door.

"Mr. Donovan?" he called into the apartment, then refocused on Billie. "Go on in. I'll keep watch through the door in case anyone shows up."

Billie wandered into the living room. Two mugs sat on the table, along with two plates of half-eaten food.

The door to the patio slid open and a blonde woman stepped inside, fiddling with her smartphone. She wore a formfitting skirt, teal blouse and high heels. She looked like she belonged here.

Billie felt like someone had punched her in the stomach. The woman frowned at her phone and glanced up, spotting Billie.

"Oh, hello," the woman said. "You must be Billie." The blonde winked. "Quinn's told me a lot about you."

"Oh really?" Billie said, crossing her arms over her chest.

The blonde's phone buzzed and she studied it.

"Mr. Donovan is coming," Joe said from the door.

Billie knew she had no claim on Quinn, that he wasn't committed to anyone but himself, but still, during the past few days she really thought they'd made progress, that he was ready to be true to his feelings for Billie and...

And what?

The apartment door opened.

"Alicia, I got some cream from the—Joe, what are you doing here?" Quinn said.

"You said if I suspected the suite had been comprised to bring her here."

"Is Billie okay?" Quinn said in a frantic voice.

"I'm fine," she called from the living room, not taking her eyes off the blonde woman.

He came into the living room and made a beeline for Billie. He reached for her, but she turned away and went to the sliding door. "I could use some air." She opened the door, wanting to escape the scene in the living room.

Alicia was beautiful, to be sure, with perfectly applied makeup that accentuated her catlike eyes. She was one of the glamorous types, like the ones Quinn used to bring home for dinner in Waverly Harbor.

"Joe, watch the hallway," Quinn said. "Alicia, I'll be right back. Make yourself at home."

Make yourself at home? Billie fumed, stepping outside onto the patio. She wanted to slam the patio door shut and take off across the property, but she wasn't a foolish woman. She wouldn't put herself at risk because she'd made a wrong assumption about Quinn. She'd thought they shared more than a dysfunctional rescuer-rescuee relationship, but apparently she was way off base.

"Billie?" Quinn said from behind her.

"I'm sorry we intruded on your privacy. Joe thought it would be best if we left my suite because I received a crank call."

She heard the slider shut and sensed him step close. "That was a good decision."

"How long do I need to stay here?"

"I'm not sure. Perhaps you should stay in my apartment permanently."

She spun around. "Are you crazy? I have enough stress

with strangers trying to hurt me. I don't need people I care about hurting me, as well."

"Billie—"

"I watched you date women in Waverly Harbor and I managed to deal with it, barely, but I managed. I told myself I was vulnerable because my husband had died and you were so generous and strong, so I developed an attachment to you. But this—" she motioned to the sliding door leading to his apartment "—this is torture, Quinn. I will not watch you march women in and out of your apartment because you're trying to drive me away again."

"You…you knew that's what I was doing?" he whispered.

"Sure, I got the message and finally left town. But now you've assigned yourself my protector and I felt like we were getting closer. I thought you'd outgrown your fear of being in a relationship with me, and now you expect me to be okay with a blonde woman in your apartment? I'm not okay, Quinn. That's certainly not okay."

She started for the door, but he blocked her. "Let me explain."

"Don't, I've heard all your lines."

"She's my cousin."

Billie snapped her attention to him.

"She texted me out of the blue last night and asked if she could swing by. She's a sales rep and was going to be calling on customers in the area. I comped her a room down the hall. We haven't spoken since before my father died."

"Oh," Billie said, feeling embarrassment color her cheeks. "Was she here when you came to check on me last night?"

"Yes."

"Why didn't you say something?"

"I didn't want you to feel bad about taking me away from my family, so I didn't mention it."

Billie glanced down at her sneakers. "Wow, talk about the world's most embarrassing moment."

"Don't be embarrassed. Everything you said was right on the mark. I brought women home to push you away, to make sure you knew what kind of man I was so you wouldn't develop an attachment to me."

Billie glanced at him. "Why?"

"You'd just lost your husband, sweetheart. You were vulnerable and I'm a selfish jerk. I didn't trust myself not to let something develop between us. I cared about you too much to allow that to happen."

"You cared about me? Back then?"

"Yes, but it was totally inappropriate."

"And now? Is it still inappropriate?" She searched his bright blue eyes.

"I don't have an answer for that."

"Maybe I do." Billie leaned forward, stood on her tiptoes and kissed him on the lips.

Warmth drifted across her body. This felt so right, so perfect, as if they were meant to kiss like this, touch like this.

Quinn's phone vibrated. He broke the kiss, pressing his forehead against hers. "We're not done...talking, but I need to get this."

"Yeah, okay." She smiled and wandered a few feet away, running her hand across the wooden railing of his patio.

"Yes, she got a crank call so she's here at my place. So that was you? Okay....I see. Sure, bye."

She turned to him. "Everything okay?"

"That was Detective Issacs. He called your room, but had a bad connection."

"So he was the crank caller? Great, I set everyone into panic mode for nothing. What did he want?"

"He had an update. The company your husband drove for, Marshall's Scrap Yard, is closed so that was a dead end."

"So we're no closer to putting an end to this, yet someone still tried to run me down at the hospital."

"Maybe they were trying to grab you, not run you down."

"Which is just as bad," she said.

"There's more. The bearded suspect they took into custody?"

"Yes?"

"He claims the head of the theft ring is an active SAR member."

ELEVEN

"No, I won't accept that," Billie said.

She considered the SAR group her family, which they were, since both her parents were gone and she didn't have aunts, uncles or cousins close by.

"I'm sorry," Quinn offered.

Billie paced a few feet away, trying to make sense of it all. An SAR member was in charge of the burglary ring? Besides church, the SAR group was the one place she felt safe, surrounded by loyal and honorable friends.

"Quinn, I can't believe it's someone so close to me."

Quinn's gentle hand touched her shoulder. "Let's talk about this inside."

She glanced at the sliding door and hesitated. "I wasn't very nice to your cousin."

"I'm sure it's not the first time she's dealt with a jealous female."

"I shouldn't have been jealous."

"At the time you didn't know she was my cousin."

"I meant, I have no right to be jealous. It's not like I have any claim over you."

Quinn studied her for a second and burst out laughing.

She stared at him, aghast. "What's so funny?"

"You have no claim over me? That's a joke, right?"

"No, I—"

He cut off her response with a kiss. Sweet, tender and full of promise. The door slid open. "Oops, sorry."

Quinn broke the kiss, leaving Billie a little off balance. When he kissed her it was as if she was transported to another place, a safe place.

"I didn't mean to interrupt," Alicia said from the door.

"It's fine, we were about to join you." Quinn slipped his fingers through Billie's and led her inside.

Billie offered Alicia an apologetic smile. "Sorry if I was rude before."

"No problem. You thought I was the competition—I get it."

"I'll make some tea." Quinn's fingers eased from Billie's and she was reluctant to let go.

"Can I help?" Billie offered.

"Don't trust me?" he winked.

Her tummy fluttered, but not because of the wink. He'd kissed her, after laughing at her comment about not having a claim on him, which meant...

She couldn't think about that now. She had to figure out which SAR member was involved in this mess. "I should head to my suite and continue my research."

"Detective Issacs wants us to let him do his job, remember?" Quinn said from the kitchen.

"I know these people better than he does. I could help."

Quinn poked his head around the corner. "I'm sure you could but how about we take it easy for a few minutes and visit with Alicia?"

"Okay, sure."

Alicia extended her hand. "Let's start over. I'm Alicia Harper, Quinn's cousin."

"Nice to meet you." Billie shook her hand and sat on the couch. Alicia joined her.

"Quinn said you two haven't seen each other in a while," Billie said.

"Years. Our families weren't close after Quinn's dad remarried. That woman was a piece of work."

"So I've heard."

The wall phone rang in the kitchen. "Hello?" Quinn's voice echoed into the living room.

Billie leaned forward. "Before when you said you've heard a lot about me, what did Quinn tell you?"

"He didn't have to tell me anything. It's obvious he's in love with you."

The women were giggling. Quinn should be glad that Billie was doing something other than hiding or running, dodging an oncoming car or…kissing him.

Man, that was incredible and unexpected. Quinn had no idea how to respond, so he kissed her back.

"Quinn? Are you listening to me?" Quinn's brother, Alex, demanded through the phone.

"Yeah, sorry."

"What's going on over there?"

"They're giggling in the living room," Quinn said.

"Alicia probably told Billie about the time you lost your trunks diving into Lake Serene."

"Thanks, that makes me feel much better."

"Ten years old and already trying to impress the ladies with your diving skills."

"I'd rather not relive that memory if it's all the same to you."

"You're right, I don't have to embarrass you since you've got Alicia there to do it. Telling your girlfriend about your most embarrassing moments as a kid."

"Billie's not—never mind. Did you call for a reason?"

"I heard you chased down and caught a viable suspect in the theft-ring case."

"What, does Issacs have you on speed dial?"

"Issacs? No. A friend with Lake Stevens P.D. called to tell me about my brave little brother."

"I'm thirty-four. I can take care of myself."

"No argument here. Only next time call the police be-fore you walk into a dangerous situation."

"I didn't know it was dangerous."

"Sounds like everything involving Billie Bronson is dangerous until this case is solved."

Quinn peered around the corner into the living room. "Yeah, sounds about right."

"Tell Alicia to swing by Waverly Harbor and I'll intro-duce her to Nicole," Alex said.

"How is your lovely fiancée?"

"She's great. Her personal-assistant business is really taking off."

"And the wedding plans?"

"Good." He paused. "They're good."

"You okay?"

"Yeah. I was just thinking how close I came to losing her."

"But you didn't. You taught her how to defend herself and she survived."

"It could have gone a completely different way," Alex said.

"But it didn't, and you're getting married."

"And hopefully you'll be right behind me."

"Come again?"

"You couldn't ask for a better woman than Billie."

"Well, there's always Nicole."

"Very funny. Look, bro, I don't want you to lose Billie because you think you can protect her by yourself. Help the police do their jobs here, Quinn. Don't play superhero."

"Thanks for the vote of confidence."

"That's not what I meant."

"Gotta go." Quinn abruptly ended the call.

He found himself doing that every once in a while when on the receiving end of a lecture from his older brother. Quinn respected Alex, but he didn't like being bossed around by a guy who barely knew him. Until this past year, Alex and Quinn had spoken infrequently and argued most of the time when they did.

Then Alex needed Quinn's help. Correction: Alex's murder witness, Nicole, had needed help and she contacted Quinn. It was the first time Alex had seen little brother Quinn as an adult, a competent man that Alex would willingly choose to take into battle.

Yet just now big brother told Quinn to ask the police for help next time before charging into a dangerous situation to protect Billie.

Hadn't Quinn said the same thing to Billie when he'd rescued her in the mountains? He told her it was okay to accept help, and it was...just not for Quinn.

He wandered into the living room and set down a tray with a teapot and three cups. "I've got milk and sugar. Alicia, need more coffee?"

"No, I'm good, thanks."

Quinn poured himself a cup of tea and sat in the recliner. Billie's cheeks were flushed red and a smile played at her lips.

"Okay, what are we talking about?" Quinn asked.

Billie looked at Alicia.

They burst out laughing.

An hour later Quinn walked his cousin out to her car. "Now I know why we never see each other," Quinn said. "My reputation can't handle it."

"Lighten up. It makes you seem more human when people know about the crazy stuff you did as a kid."

"I'd say it makes me look downright insane." They reached her car and he opened the door.

She hesitated before getting behind the wheel. "She's really nice, Quinn."

"Yeah, too nice for me," he joked.

Alicia wasn't smiling. "Don't let her do that."

"What?"

"Don't let the stepmonster ruin this for you."

"I don't know what—"

"She doesn't matter, Quinn. All that horrible stuff she said to you, it's meaningless, done. Let it go."

"I thought I had."

Alicia gave him a hug and got in the car. "Behave."

"You're kidding, right?"

"Always the jokester."

"Say hi to Alex for me." He shut the door and watched her drive off.

He and Alicia had seen each other only a few times as adults. This time felt different. They'd made a real connection and he suspected Billie was responsible for that. Billie and her positive, hopeful energy.

Practically jogging back to his apartment, he flung open the door. "So are you still talking to me?"

The living room was empty.

"Billie?"

She popped her head through the kitchen doorway. She was on the floor.

"What's wrong?" he said, rushing to her side.

She kneeled in front of a cupboard, pulling out boxes of dried food. "This pasta expired in 2012. And this one—" she held up a box of rice "—December of 2011." She pulled out cans and placed them above her on the counter.

"Billie, come on, we don't have to do this now." He offered his hand, but she ignored it.

"You could get sick from two-year-old canned chili. We can't risk that. Your life is dangerous enough because you're watching out for me. You shouldn't increase your risk by keeping this stuff around."

He sat down next to her on the floor. This was not about expired pasta. "You're absolutely right," he said. "Thanks for going through my cupboards, but we have other things we should be focusing on."

She glanced at him with her big, brown eyes. "This is important, Quinn. Rancid food in your stomach could cause all kinds of problems—parasites, and cramping and all kinds of illness."

"Billie?" He touched her hand, resting on her thigh. "Why do we have to do this now?"

Her gaze drifted to his hand. "Because I can do something here, I can throw out expired food. It's the only thing I have control over. I couldn't control what my husband did or someone trying to run me down and nearly killing Bree. I can't control the fact that an SAR member, someone I trust with my life, is involved in this conspiracy." She glanced at her other hand, clutching a can of soup. "But I can toss the chicken and dumpling soup before it kills you."

"Okay, then let's do this." Quinn shifted beside her and helped her pull more cans and boxes out of the cabinet. He wanted to focus on their investigation, but figured another half hour wouldn't make a big difference. It seemed obvious that throwing stuff out would ease Billie's anxiety and give her a sense of control, something she'd been lacking since the day she was assaulted on the trail.

She paused for a second and glanced at him. "Thank you."

"For what? You're saving my life, remember?" Offering a charming smile, he continued analyzing expiration dates.

He meant it. She was saving his life, and not by throwing out expired stews and soups. Billie was saving Quinn's life in ways she couldn't possibly imagine.

They sorted and tossed expired food for the next forty-five minutes until she seemed satisfied that Quinn wouldn't get sick from eating canned pineapple dated August 2010.

He escorted her to her suite and Joe, who'd been standing guard outside Quinn's door, followed close behind.

"Sorry I overreacted this morning about the phone call," she said.

"You didn't," Quinn said. "I would have made the same assumption."

"You're just saying that to be nice."

"Ouch," he said, gripping his chest. "My ego took a serious hit."

Joe chuckled behind them.

"I meant it as a compliment," she protested.

"Okay, well, thanks for that," Quinn said.

"But don't call him nice ever again," Joe added.

"Okay," she said with a smile.

She swiped her keycard and opened the door to her suite. She hesitated before stepping inside.

"What is it?" Quinn asked.

"I'm embarrassed that it's such a mess."

He motioned her into the room. "It's a hotel room. Housekeeping is supposed to clean the room, not the guest."

Quinn wandered to the window and gazed across the surrounding property. If someone knew Billie was staying in this room, it would be easy enough to pick a spot in the forest bordering the resort and watch her through a telescopic lens. He made a mental note to have Hank send a few guys out there to check.

As Quinn scanned the property, he heard Billie shuffling papers behind him. "I'll have housekeeping swing by in the next hour to clean up. Get your paperwork together and we'll go through it at my place," Quinn said.

"Where is it?" she said.

He turned to her, noting her frantic search of the desk. "Where's what?"

"A topographic map. It was right on top of this pile and it's gone." She took a step back from the desk and glanced at Quinn with fear in her eyes. "Someone was in my room."

Quinn put his forefinger to his lips, tiptoed to the closet

and kept talking. "You probably misplaced the map. Check the box."

He whipped open the closet door. Empty.

Motioning her to stay back, he went into the bedroom, but it was empty. If the intruder were still in the suite it could end the speculation about the SAR member's identity.

He swung open the bedroom closet. No one was hiding in there either. He checked the window in her bedroom—securely locked.

Quinn went into the living room. "No one's here," he said, checking the sliding door to the patio. It opened with ease. "But this is how they got access to your room."

He glanced at Billie. She'd wrapped her arms around her middle and stood very still. "Someone was in my room…" she hesitated "…touching…my stuff."

Fear colored her normally gentle eyes and it tore him apart.

"Hey, honey, it's okay." He crossed the room and pulled her into a hug, angry that an intruder made her feel so vulnerable. "We'd better move you."

She searched his eyes. "Move me where?"

"My apartment. It's got a security system independent of the resort, plus motion sensors outside. You'll be safe there."

"Where will you stay?"

He shoved back the pain lancing through his chest. "I'll secure a room down the hall."

"Oh, okay," she said, reaching for his hand.

When she made contact he thought he'd fall apart. This amazing woman was touching him, but couldn't stand the thought of sharing living space. That didn't bode well for a future together. A future? Wait, what was he thinking about?

Someone knocked at the door. Quinn slipped his hand from hers and opened the door to Aiden.

"I stopped by to check on Billie. Is everything okay?"

Quinn motioned Aiden into the room. "We had a scare

this morning. She got a crank call so the security guard brought her to my apartment. While she was at my place, someone got into her room and stole documents."

"Got into her room, how?"

"Sliding door."

"That's not possible. You can't unlock it from the outside."

"Which means—" Quinn glanced at Billie "—someone was in your room earlier and unlocked the door with plans to return later. Make a list of all your visitors since you've been staying here."

"Maybe someone in housekeeping left it open," Aiden offered.

"More likely it was someone from SAR. Detective Issacs said the leader of this theft ring is on the SAR team."

"Not possible," Aiden countered. "We know everyone in SAR. They're good people, Quinn."

"I didn't believe it either at first," Billie offered. "But now…" She glanced at the sliding door.

"Perhaps you forgot to lock the slider last night," Aiden said.

"I haven't touched that door since I've been here. I didn't want to risk it."

"So what do we do?" Aiden said.

"I'll set her up in my place. Can you get me a room close by?"

"Sure. I'll juggle some stuff around. We've got a big tour group coming in tonight and need to book rooms in this wing."

"No," Quinn said.

"I've got no other place to put them."

"I don't care."

"We're talking four grand worth of revenue," Aiden countered.

All Quinn could think about was hundreds of strangers added to the mix of an already volatile situation.

"Quinn," Billie said. "I will not allow my situation to compromise the resort's financial stability. Let Aiden book the rooms."

Quinn sighed. He knew that Billie didn't need one more thing to feel guilty about, and turning away thousands of dollars would certainly make her feel even worse.

"Fine, but first, let's get Billie moved into my apartment."

Billie spent a solid four hours going through paperwork the intruder hadn't taken and analyzing the list of SAR members for any red flags, as Quinn put it. Aiden had provided the list, and also emailed a copy to Detective Issacs.

Quinn had a whiteboard delivered to his apartment and suggested Billie list all the SAR members and write down everything she knew about them. She hesitated when writing Will's name on the board, not wanting the gentle single father to be involved in this.

She'd been praying for Will regularly since his wife died, hoping he'd find strength in God's word and not let grief over losing his wife turn into bitterness.

But sometimes grief had a way of turning into anger or resentment. Will was friendly most of the time, but once in a while he seemed withdrawn. Sometimes she wondered how he managed being on the SAR team while raising two little girls and running his computer business. Luckily his career allowed him a flexible schedule working from home.

Speaking of which, she glanced across the living room at Quinn. He was sitting at the kitchen counter working on his laptop, keeping his distance to let her concentrate.

After lunch, Quinn encouraged Billie to take a nap in the guest room, and she didn't argue. The constant adrenaline spikes, coupled with her minor injuries from the fall, sapped her usual resilience.

Two hours later she awakened, wandered into the living room and found Quinn asleep on the sofa in a sitting position, his hands folded comfortably in his lap. Not wanting to wake him, she tiptoed into the kitchen for a glass of water.

"Good nap?" he said.

She peeked her head around the corner. "Pretty good, yeah. I'm getting water, want some?"

"No thanks."

She wandered into the living room, sipping her water.

"I touched base with Cody. He's being released today," Quinn said.

"That's great news. How's he feeling?"

"A little sore, but that's to be expected." He nodded at the flow chart she'd made earlier. "Any obvious suspects from the SAR list?"

"Not really. No one person stands out as suffering from undue financial stress more than another. They've all gone through their share of challenges these past few years."

"Thanks to the plant closing, I know."

"Well, and other things, not just the plant." She fingered the rim of her glass. "Quinn, thank you for offering your apartment while you stay down the hall."

"My pleasure. I understand your need for distance."

"What do you mean?"

"It's hard being around me so much. I mean, you know the reality of our situation, what kind of man I am—"

"Yes, Quinn, I do. But I don't think you have a clue."

"I've lived with myself for thirty-four years. I think I know myself pretty well."

"Oh really." Billie smiled. "Tell me more."

"You love teasing me."

No, I just love you.

Billie felt her smile fade as reality struck her hard in the chest. She glanced away.

"I'm guessing a lot of women jumped at the chance to share living space with you," she said.

"I'm not comfortable talking about this."

"Come on. How many actually got a key?"

"One. My wife. That's it."

She snapped her attention to him, shocked. He must have read the disbelief in her eyes.

"Reputations aren't always reflective of the truth," he said.

"When you invited women to your lake house in Waverly Harbor, I assumed they spent the night."

"They didn't. I always drove them home."

"What about the one from Seattle?"

"Katrina? I drove her to the Waverly Inn."

"I don't understand."

"Many of them were business associates, others I enjoyed spending time with, but I'd never let any of them get close enough to destroy me."

"Quinn, you make it sound like all women are your mortal enemies."

"Not all women." He glanced up and his expression softened, snagging her heart.

She couldn't speak, couldn't articulate a pithy, clever retort.

"Hungry?" he said, standing.

But her brain was hooked on what he'd just said: Had he confessed that he didn't consider Billie the enemy? That she was different than the rest of the women in his life? She was still trying to process the fact he didn't let any of his female guests spend the night.

"I can order burgers and fries from room service," he said, consulting a resort menu.

Shouting in the hallway echoed through the door. Quinn eyed the peephole. "Sounds like they're headed down for the luau." He glanced at Billie. "Aiden texted me that it's Hawaiian night in the dining room."

Hawaiian night with live entertainment, kebabs, fresh fruit and coconut pudding. The resort hosted one six months ago and it had been a big hit. Billie acted as one of the greeters and thoroughly enjoyed watching the guests celebrate with their families.

"Would you rather have fish?" Quinn asked.

"Actually…" She stood and crossed the room to him. "Is there any chance we could go to the dining room?"

"Not a chance, sweetheart," he said, studying the menu.

"Quinn, I could use a break from the intensity of the past few days. No one's going to expect me to be in a public place and even so, they wouldn't risk coming after me with all those people around. You and Joe will be right beside me. Come on, please?"

He glanced at her and shook his head. "Like I could ever say no to you. Fine. Against my better judgment, we'll go, but only for an hour."

She kissed him on the cheek and ran toward the guest room to change. "I've got a floral shirt in here somewhere."

Ten minutes later she was literally flanked by Quinn and Joe as they escorted her to the dining room.

Quinn led them to a table in the corner. Billie smiled with delight as she watched the hoop-twirling contest. "I could do that," she shouted over the music, then caught Quinn's scowl. "But I'll pass."

The server took their order and Billie's mouth watered at the thought of ham and pineapple kebabs and sweet potatoes.

She caught Quinn studying her and she smiled, thrilled to be out among people acting like a normal person instead of a target. Bree drifted to their table and kneeled beside her. "Two dates, not bad!" she teased. "I'm gonna try hooping, wanna come?"

"No thanks. I'll cheer you on!"

Bree took off for the center of the dance floor and some-one handed her a hoop. Quinn stood and pointed at his phone. "Can't hear! I'm taking this outside!"

Billie nodded. Quinn aimed an index finger at Joe, who saluted his understanding: keep Billie safe.

Bree was having a ball, swinging her hips and laughing at herself and her competition, which included a few teen-agers, senior citizens and even a toddler.

And for a few minutes, all of Billie's anxiety and worry left her mind and her body. She soaked in the laughter and music, and took a mental picture of this joyous scene to re-member if she felt down in the future.

She smiled and leaned against her chair. She felt relaxed. Normal.

Suddenly the piercing sound of a fire alarm cut through the music. Dining room guests rushed off the dance floor. Aiden tried calming them via the PA system, but he couldn't be heard over the frantic blare of the alarm.

Joe grabbed Billie's arm and pulled her toward the crowd. Someone bumped into her on the right and she stumbled. Joe suddenly let go and they got separated. Shoved left, then right, Billie crossed her arms over her chest to protect her bruised ribs, and she pretended to be a linebacker for the Seattle Seahawks.

But she wasn't a six-foot, three-hundred-pound football player. Billie was petite and barely five four. Jostled one way, then the other, anxiety knotted her stomach as she fo-cused on remaining calm.

Someone slammed her against the wall.

She gasped.

A firm hand gripped her arm and yanked her into the kitchen.

TWELVE

Heart racing, Billie staggered into the abandoned kitchen and tugged free of her attacker. She grabbed a knife off the counter, spun around and pointed it at—

Will.

The fire alarm clicked off, blanketing them in eerie silence.

Will put out his hands. "Sorry, but you looked like you were in trouble."

"I was, I am. Why did you bring me in here?"

"You were being shoved back and forth. You seemed freaked out and this was the closest door to get you away from the crowd." He lowered his hands.

Billie didn't lower the knife. Adrenaline hijacked her mind and wasn't letting go.

"Aren't you supposed to have a twenty-four-hour guard?" Will said. "What about Donovan? Where is he?"

"Why do you want to know?" Suspicion tickled her senses. Or was it fear?

"I'm worried about you." He shoved his hands into his pockets.

Will had a sweet, boy-next-door face, which usually put her at ease. Yet Quinn's words haunted her: *People aren't always what they seem on the outside.*

"Look, I'm trying to help," he offered.

"Why?"

"You're my friend. You've always been there to help me

with the girls. I feel so inadequate without Megan," he said, glancing at the floor. A few seconds passed and he cleared his throat. "You looked terrified in the dining room. My instinct was to protect you." He eyed the knife. "I realize you've been through a lot but I'm not the enemy, Billie."

She slowly lowered the knife. Was she crazy? Threatening Will with a weapon she never intended to use?

"It's his influence, isn't it?" Will said.

"What? Whose influence?"

"Donovan. He's taught you to be cynical and suspicious of everyone, even your friends."

"No, it's this case." She placed the knife in the sink. "I don't know who to trust anymore."

"But you trust him?" His voice cracked. "I don't get it. He's a ruthless businessman and, from what I hear, a womanizer. Why would you trust a man like that?"

"You don't know him."

"I know enough." He shook his head.

Shame tweaked her chest and she didn't like it.

"You may be my friend, Will, but that doesn't give you the right to judge me or my decisions. I know Quinn, the real Quinn, not the man everyone else thinks they know. I'm disappointed that you wouldn't trust my judgment." She turned to leave.

"Wait, Billie?"

She hesitated.

"You're right, I'm sorry. I guess, well, you're a bright woman. You must have figured out that if there's anyone in Echo Mountain I'd love to be in my girls' life permanently, it's you."

Billie sighed. She turned to him and smiled. "I'm honored, truly."

"But your heart belongs to someone else?"

"As does yours. Don't rush things. When you're ready I'm sure the perfect woman will walk into your life."

"What if she already has?"

She motioned to him. "Come on, let's get out of here."

With a nod, he crossed the room. She slipped her arm through his and they left the kitchen to join the others outside.

They wandered through the empty hallway and out the front door where guests gathered a safe distance from the building. She'd been so worried about who'd grabbed her that she'd completely blocked out the reason for the commotion: a fire.

She spotted Quinn racing toward them. She smiled, anticipating a relieved hug. Instead, he ignored her, grabbed Will and shoved him against a nearby post.

"Quinn, stop!" Billie said, but it didn't seem to faze him.

"Who are you working for?" Quinn accused.

"I'm not—"

"How did you know she'd be in the dining room? Were you stalking her? Hanging around the resort until she came out of her room?"

"Quinn." Billie gripped his muscled arm. "Look at me."

"I want to know who sent you. What's his name?" Quinn demanded.

"I don't know what you're talking about. I stopped by the SAR building to drop off equipment."

"And found your way inside the resort and, what, went looking for Billie?"

"Donovan!" Detective Issacs rushed toward them.

Billie noticed Aiden direct the guests back into the resort.

"I saw that Billie was in trouble and went to help," Will said.

"I'll bet you did," Quinn ground out.

"And where were you? Isn't it your job to protect her?" Quinn fisted his right hand.

"Quinn, look at me," Billie demanded.

Clenching his jaw, his fist poised to strike, he glanced down at Billie.

"I'm fine. I'm safe. Let him go." She didn't break eye contact, even though the intensity of his blue eyes could have burned her to ash where she stood. He was insanely worried about her, and probably furious with himself for leaving her alone.

"That's enough." Detective Issacs shoved Quinn away. "I've got this. Will Rankin, I need you to come with me."

"What, why?"

"I need to ask you some questions."

"About what?"

"We can talk about that at the station. Come on," Detective Issacs motioned him to the car.

Will didn't move. His face drained of color.

"Or do I need to officially arrest you?" Issacs pressed.

With a stupefied expression, Will glanced at Billie. "You know I'd never do anything to hurt you."

"I know."

Another officer led Will to a waiting squad car.

"The candy was spiked with diazepam," the detective said to Billie. "Not lethal but it would have knocked you out. We got a partial print off the card." He turned and headed to the squad car.

At least most of the guests had gone back inside and didn't witness Will being escorted away. She worried about locals seeing the exchange, which could ignite the gossip mill.

"Inside, now," Quinn snapped at Billie.

She slowly redirected her gaze from Will to Quinn. "Check your tone, Quinn. I realize that you're upset, but that doesn't give you the right to speak to me that way." She spotted her security guard standing a few feet away. "Joe, can you escort me to Quinn's—to my quarters?"

"Of course."

She walked away from Quinn, giving him space to calm down. She understood he was frustrated, but why take it out on Will?

Will. Now she'd dragged *him* into this mess simply because he was trying to help her. What did the detective want with him, anyway?

She should be relieved that the chocolates sent to her room didn't contain poison. Yet they were spiked with a sedative, which meant what? They wanted her to pass out so they could kidnap her?

Her mind spinning with questions, she hesitated in front of room 118.

"Down here, remember?" Joe said, motioning to Quinn's apartment door.

"Oh, right."

She was rattled, first by all the pushing and shoving, then being yanked into the kitchen and finally by Quinn's violent behavior. She'd never seen him like that before, not even when his big brother got in his face and challenged him in ways no one else dared. Quinn would click on the aloof persona and smile, but it wasn't real. She could sense the real smiles from the pretend ones.

Joe swiped the keycard and they went into the apartment. He pressed the keypad deactivating the security system so another alarm didn't go off. She'd had enough of blaring alarms, panic, confusion and noise.

She went directly to the guest room and shut the door, closing herself off from the rest of the world. With a sigh, she flopped down on the bed and stared at the ceiling. Maybe she shouldn't have turned away from Quinn so abruptly and left him standing there, but she didn't know what else to do.

Feeling anxious and frustrated, she decided to read to distract herself. She glanced left at the bookshelf and her eyes widened. There was actually a Bible sitting on the shelf. She rolled off the bed and stared at the bookshelf, thinking maybe she'd imagined it. She pulled it off the shelf, cracked it open and began reading to calm herself.

An hour later someone tapped on her door, probably Joe wanting to see if she needed anything. Her tummy growled and she realized she hadn't eaten much when they'd gone down for the luau.

She climbed off the bed and opened the door. No one was there, but soft tones of a ukulele drifted through the apartment.

"Hello?" she said, stepping into the living room.

A bouquet of flowers was at the center of the coffee table and colorful paper flowers hung from the ceiling. The aroma of the freshly cut flowers was almost as good as whatever was simmering on the stove. She went into the kitchen and found Quinn, wearing a BBQ apron, stirring something in a big stainless-steel pot.

He glanced at her. "I thought you might be hungry."

She was glad he chose not to talk about what happened in the parking lot, but she knew they couldn't avoid it forever.

"I am, thanks. What's for dinner?" she said.

"Barbeque pork, sweet potatoes, coconut lime skewers and spaghetti." He nodded at the pot.

"Spaghetti?"

"Wanted to cover all my bases, in case something didn't turn out." He flipped off the burner. "Oh, and we've got entertainment."

He motioned her into the living room and clicked on the flat screen. They were watching guests dancing in the decorated dining room on the closed-circuit TV.

"They didn't cancel the luau?" she said.

"No, ma'am, and I didn't want you to miss out on the fun, even if you can't be there in person."

"Thanks, I—"

A timer went off in the kitchen. "Hold that thought." He rushed into the kitchen.

She smiled. He'd done all this to make up for being a jerk before, threatening Will and snapping at Billie.

Following him into the kitchen, she said, "I'm worried about Will."

He handed her plates and utensils. "Can you set the table?"

"Quinn, do you know why the detective wanted to speak with him?"

Quinn shrugged. "Not sure. I guess he made the suspect list."

"No, not Will. He's got two little girls, and he'd never do anything to hurt me."

"Go sit down. I'll bring the food out."

Billie went to the dining table and pulled out a chair. She couldn't believe Will was involved in a theft ring. She worried that being brought in for questioning would threaten his relationship with the girls. Billie had heard rumors that his in-laws had never fully approved of Will, and Megan had married him against their wishes. Billie hoped they didn't use this incident as an excuse to try to get custody of the children.

"I'm sure if he's not involved Detective Issacs won't detain him," Quinn offered.

He must have sensed what she was thinking and was trying to ease her worry. Quinn set platters of food on the table, took off his apron and joined her.

"It's beautiful, Quinn. I'm very grateful." She interlaced her fingers and said a silent prayer.

"If you want…" he hesitated "…you can say it aloud." He studied her hands, as if figuring out how to appropriately put his hands together in prayer.

She warmed at the thought that he was trying to open his heart to God.

"Okay," she said. "God is good, God is great, we thank Him for our food. Amen."

"Amen," Quinn said. "Hope you're hungry."

"I am, thanks."

"I'll serve. What looks good?"

"Everything."

"Good, so my plan worked." He placed a kebab on her plate.

"What plan?"

"Butter you up with food so you'll talk to me. I was a jerk in the parking lot." He spooned some barbeque pork. "Want this as a sandwich? I have rolls in the kitchen."

"I'll start with the kebab, thanks." She studied him. "Can I ask you something?"

He smiled as he served himself pork. "Do I have to answer?"

"Only if you want to."

"Now there's a mine field if I've ever heard one," he joked.

"Why were you so crazed in the parking lot? I mean, you saw that I was okay, that I was unharmed and safe yet your tone of voice…" She shook her head.

He slowly returned the spoon to the pork dish. "You really want me to answer that?"

"Yes, please."

When he glanced into her eyes, the vulnerability she read there made her want to look away because it felt as if she was seeing something so incredibly private and painful, but she didn't dare break eye contact.

"I was insane," he started, "out of my mind at the thought of you being stalked while trying to get out of the dining room. If anything had happened to you…" His voice trailed off. He shook his head and glanced down at his food.

She reached for his hand and clasped it between her

own. "Nothing happened. I'm okay. And I'm here, safe in your apartment."

"Yeah, but when I didn't know where you were or who you were with…" He hesitated. "I was stuck outside trying to get into the building. Aiden was restraining me, and I was shouting your name. I almost slugged him to get away so I could find you. He told me no one was allowed inside until the alarm stopped, which only made me more crazy."

"Thank you, Quinn."

He glanced at her. "For being crazy?"

"For caring as much as you do."

"I'm surprised you're thanking me. I was pretty rough on your boyfriend."

"Boyfriend? You mean Will?"

"It's obvious he's got a thing for you."

"It's a one-sided thing." Still holding Quinn's hand, she nibbled at a chicken skewer.

"I had Alex do a background check and Will came out clean. Before tonight I thought Will would be a good catch."

"This coming from the guy who wanted to punch his lights out in the parking lot?"

"Like I said, I was crazed. I'm okay now. I've embraced the reality of the situation." He pulled his hand from hers.

"And what reality is that?"

"That after everything you've been through, you deserve a good man in your life. A guy with integrity, someone solid and dependable."

"Funny, those are all adjectives I'd use to describe you."

"You're just being nice because I made you dinner."

"No, Quinn, I mean it. You're one of the best men I know."

Speechless, Quinn glanced down at his plate. For an awkward few seconds he felt her gaze on him and wondered how she could see things in him that no one else could. There was a strange but amazing connection between them, a connection that touched him on a visceral level.

Luckily the closed-circuit coverage of the luau snagged her attention. "They're adorable," she said, watching a group of little girls compete in a coconut-decorating contest.

Quinn was awed by the joy he read on Billie's face. She'd be an amazing mother someday.

Sadness settled low in his gut. There'd been no role model in his life, no supportive and nurturing parent, so he wouldn't have a clue how to effectively raise a child. He'd surely never risk foisting his lack of experience on his own kid.

They spent the next few hours eating and talking about the case, and their lives. It was as if they existed in a safe bubble, free of judgment or threat. Was this what unconditional love felt like?

As she helped him with the dishes, he found himself dreading the moment she'd head into the guest room, leaving him alone with his thoughts.

Selfish jerk. She was probably exhausted and needed to turn in. He caught her covering a yawn with her hand.

"Go to bed. I'll finish cleaning up," he offered.

"You sure?"

"Absolutely. I'll see you in the morning."

"Sunday. Church." She smiled.

"I have a little work I'll finish up here in the apartment tonight."

"Okay."

They ambled into the living room. She paused and turned to him. "Good night." She slipped her arms around his waist in a loving embrace and he realized his arms naturally held on to her, as well. They stood there for a good ten seconds, his hand trailing up her back to stroke her hair.

She suddenly let go, went into the guest room and shut the door.

He had the sudden urge to grab his laptop and camp out on the floor outside her door.

"Not good, Donovan, really not good," he muttered.

He was falling in love with a woman he could never be with, a woman he would abandon once the threat against her life was gone. That's what you did if you truly cared about someone: you made her needs a priority.

Billie needed stability and the promise of a future with a devoted husband and children—the antithesis of Quinn Donovan. He could only hope she'd accept that reality before she accidentally fell in love with him.

The next morning Billie's words still hummed against his chest: *You're one of the best men I know.*

The memory made him uncomfortable and proud at the same time. He decided to live up to her high opinion of him by making sure she got to church safely.

Not that he'd join her inside the house of worship. She might believe Quinn an admirable guy, but God knew the truth. A rogue like Quinn didn't belong in church. Today's security guard, Phil, followed alongside them, eyeing the crowd for suspicious activity.

Quinn spotted the McBride family—Aiden, Bree, younger sister Cassandra, and their mom, Margaret—in the parking lot. Good, Billie would have someone to sit with during the service. They all greeted one another.

"You sure you don't want to join us?" she asked Quinn.

"No, I've got—" he motioned to his phone "—business."

"Okay, see you in a bit." With a gentle smile, Billie turned and went into the church with the McBrides. Her security guard trailed close behind.

Quinn ambled to his car and leaned against the hood. His gaze took in the beautiful brick building with stained glass and he wondered what it felt like to be inside with friends and family. His brother regularly attended church and relied on God for strength, yet God had always been a mystery to Quinn.

Nearly an hour later he'd gone through emails and looked over a few properties for sale in search of business opportunities. What he guessed was the final song sounded from inside the church. Quinn closed his eyes, tipped his face to the sun and let the music wash over him. The deep tones of the organ felt grounding, yet uplifting. He could see how the music touched one's soul.

His peaceful moment was interrupted by a text message. The sheriff's department had received an emergency call and needed search-and-rescue teams to assemble at a trailhead about fifteen miles away. Good thing the service was almost over since Quinn figured about twenty of the local SAR members attended this church.

His phone rang and he answered.

"Donovan."

"Quinn, how's it goin'?" Alex said.

"It's goin'."

"That good, huh?"

"It's frustrating."

"But Billie's okay?"

"She's fine." *More than fine.*

"So are you frustrated with the case or with something else?"

"To what are you referring, big brother?" Quinn teased, knowing where Alex was headed. Quinn glanced across the parking lot at the church.

And spotted a tall man dressed in a camouflage jacket peeking in a side window.

"Hey!" Quinn called out.

"Quinn?" Alex said.

Quinn pocketed his phone. "Excuse me!"

The guy spun around, spotted Quinn and took off for a nearby car.

Quinn sprinted after him. Why was the guy running unless he had something to hide?

The front doors of the church flung open and out of the corner of his eye Quinn spotted folks casually wandering out. Camouflage guy cranked the engine of his sedan. Quinn sprinted between cars hoping to get a license plate number.

Quinn was closing in, about five car lengths away. He veered between a minivan and SUV, slid over the hood of a station wagon and got to the guy's sedan just as he was pulling away.

Quinn chased after him, focusing on getting a plate number. He was close, maybe five feet away.

The sedan stopped short but Quinn couldn't stop his momentum.

He flew onto the trunk of the car.

The car squealed into Reverse and Quinn found himself clinging to the trunk or risk falling off and being flattened.

"Quinn!" Billie cried.

The car slammed on the brakes and Quinn went flying.

THIRTEEN

Disbelief and anger rushed through Quinn as he hit the ground and rolled a few times to help absorb the impact of the fall. When he came to a stop, he couldn't breathe.

He heard the car tear off and someone shouted, "Call 9-1-1!"

"I'm an EMT. Let me through," another person said.

Quinn gasped a few times, filling his lungs. "Billie" was all he could get out.

Her beautiful face came into focus and he relaxed, but only for a second. "License plate." He struggled to stand.

"Easy," a thirtyish woman said. "I'm an EMT. Remain still, please." She took his pulse and fired off questions, probably trying to determine the seriousness of a potential head injury.

"I need to get the plate number of the car." He wavered as he tried to stand, adrenaline still rushing through his body. Or was it something more serious?

A firm but gentle hand pressed against his shoulder. "Aiden's on it. I want you to relax. Please?" Billie said with tear-filled eyes.

With a nod, he collapsed on the ground and closed his eyes, wanting to wipe the image of Billie's tears out of his mind. He couldn't stand the thought he was responsible for making her cry. Her hand remained firmly on his shoulder, the solid pressure calming his rapid heartbeat.

"I got the license plate," Aiden said.

Before Quinn could respond, Billie said, "Call Detective Issacs."

"What's his number?" Aiden asked.

Without opening his eyes, Quinn pulled out his phone and handed it to Billie. "It's in my contacts."

When she took it from him, he felt her fingers trembling against his hand. He opened his eyes and watched her pass the phone to Aiden. Then she glanced at Quinn. A tear trailed down her cheek. He reached out and brushed it away with his thumb.

"I'm fine, really."

She leaned into his touch and closed her eyes. Then, as if she realized they had an audience, she took a quick breath and leaned away from him. "Why were you chasing that guy?"

"He was hovering outside of church."

"He could have been looking for someone else."

"I couldn't take that chance."

"So you charged his car?"

"You make me sound like a mad bull."

"Don't joke about this, Quinn," she said.

"Can't help it. I guess I'm embarrassed."

"Embarrassed about what?"

"Ambulance is here!" a woman called out.

Quinn didn't know how many people had gathered around, but he was pretty sure it was a few dozen, if not more. Church is supposed to be a peaceful place, yet today thanks to Quinn it had turned ugly and violent.

He closed his eyes again, wanting to block everything out, including the shame of letting a potential suspect get away.

"Sir, can you open your eyes?" a man said.

Quinn did as requested. As they checked him out, he felt Billie's hand slip off his shoulder. He grabbed it before she could pull away.

"We need to place you on the backboard to transport you to the hospital."

"I don't need to go to the hospital."

"Please, Quinn?" Billie said, wiping another tear from her cheek.

Barely able to speak past the emotion clogging his throat, he offered a nod and closed his eyes.

Quinn heard a woman's voice, her soft whisper calming him as he awoke from a nasty dream. He didn't open his eyes at first, wanting to enjoy it a little longer, letting it ease the knot of anxiety from his chest.

It was just a dream, nothing more, a vivid dream of being hit by the black sedan. As he lay immobilized and helpless he could do nothing but watch as the sedan chased Billie through a barren field, out of sight...

"Heavenly Father," a voice whispered.

Billie was praying for him. Quinn opened his eyes to get his bearings. He spotted his favorite print on the wall, an evening scene of Paris. He was in his Echo Mountain Resort apartment. Right, E.R. doctors had given him a clean bill of health and had sent him home—a good thing since his accident had monopolized the attention of friends like Aiden who should have been out on the SAR mission.

"You're awake," Billie said.

He turned his head to the right. She sat beside him, clasping his hand between hers.

"What time is it?" he said, his voice sounding weak.

"Three. You slept for two hours."

Someone knocked on the door. She stood, but he wouldn't let go of her hand. "Don't."

"It's probably Detective Issacs or your brother."

"Alex?"

"I thought he should know what happened."

Quinn released her and sat up. "Great."

She went to the door, eyed the peephole and welcomed their guest.

"Detective Issacs, come in."

The detective strode into the living room and approached Quinn. "How are you feeling?"

"A little groggy, but I'm okay. Did you find the black sedan?"

"We found the car, not the driver. It had been reported stolen late last night and was abandoned in Lake Stevens."

"Another dead end," Quinn said.

"Maybe not. Forensics will dust for prints. I'm guessing someone's desperate if they're sending a man to find Mrs. Bronson in such a public place."

"Please call me Billie," she said.

"What about the bearded guy?" Quinn pushed. "Anything new from him?"

"Hiding behind his lawyer."

"So we're back to nowhere." Quinn stood and paced to the sliding glass door, running a frustrated hand through his hair.

"I wish we knew what they were after," Billie said.

"They want information, it's always about information," Issacs said. "Billie, what do you know that could either help or ruin their operation?"

"I have no idea."

"Think," Issacs snapped.

"Hey, back off." Quinn glared at the detective. "She would have told you by now if she knew anything that might help."

"No, it's okay," Billie said. "He's right. I've got to know something or have something they want. What about the jewels we found in the pantry?"

"They weren't worth much, so I doubt that's the reason they keep pursuing you." Detective Issacs sighed. "I'm sorry if I sound gruff. I'm frustrated and I want to close this case before more people get hurt."

Billie glanced at Quinn with sadness in her eyes. "I want that even more than you do, detective."

"Tell us what you got from the suspect and maybe that will help Billie remember something." Quinn ambled to the dining table and sat down. He was feeling a little off balance from the hit-and-run.

Billie and the detective joined him at the table.

"He was trying to negotiate a deal," Issacs started. "He said he'd give us names of everyone involved in the theft ring in exchange for no jail time."

"He shot Cody Monroe," Quinn protested.

"I know, I know. There was no way he'd avoid jail time. He figured that out, but was stalling for some reason. I'm guessing that's why he gave us Will Rankin's name."

"Will would never be involved in something illegal," Billie argued.

Quinn recognized respect in her voice when she spoke of Will.

"We know that now, but we had to question him," Issacs said.

"But he's been cleared?"

"Yes, ma'am. Cleared and back home with his children."

"As it should be." Billie crossed her arms over her chest.

Quinn read so much confidence in her body language, like she knew Will and trusted him completely.

"Since the perp's not talking, I'm trying to find pressure points like family or friends. It's always about leverage," Issacs said.

"What can we do to help?" Billie offered.

"Don't take this the wrong way, but stay out of trouble." He glanced briefly at Quinn, then redirected his attention to Billie. "Keep going through your records, old emails, anything that can expose more of the players. Try to remember things your husband said to you during the last few months of his life that seemed odd or out of character."

"We had drifted apart quite a bit." Billie glanced down as if she were ashamed.

Quinn automatically reached out and touched her hand.

Detective Issacs raised an eyebrow at the intimate gesture. Quinn ignored him. There was no reason to hide his feelings for Billie. He cared about her and didn't want her feeling ashamed or responsible for her husband's spiral into a criminal lifestyle. Besides, if anyone was responsible for sending him down that dark path it was Quinn.

"Even the most obscure comment could lead us in the right direction to finding the mastermind behind this operation," Issacs said.

"Are we thinking this is about stolen property or something more?" Quinn said.

"You mean like drugs?"

Quinn nodded.

"Doesn't look like it, but one victim claimed the burglars stole half a million dollars in bearer bonds from her wall safe. Those weren't in the storage locker or the perp's residence. We suspect either your husband had them in his possession and didn't know it, or he was keeping a little something for himself and died before the others figured out where he'd hidden his personal stash."

"Why is this happening a year after Rick's death?" Billie asked.

"Who knows, maybe they couldn't find you after you moved away. Or maybe they were waiting to cash in the bearer bonds and didn't know they were missing."

"So that's what you think they're after, the bearer bonds?" Quinn clarified.

"They're after anything Rick Bronson kept for himself," Issacs said.

"I need this to be over. I'm going to work in my room." She stood, grabbed the box off the end table and walked away.

* * *

Billie felt a meltdown coming on so she escaped into her room where she wouldn't embarrass herself in front of Quinn and the detective. As she paged through an old photo album she remarked how foreign it all seemed, as if she was leafing through someone else's life. The smiles brightening hers and Rick's faces, the playful exchanges caught by the digital camera was not at all how she remembered their last year together.

She was supposed to remember something Rick said to her, something that would enlighten investigators and end this nightmare, yet they had rarely spoken those last few months.

She flipped a page and came across a photo of her and Rick hiking in the Northern Cascades. They'd decided to hike the rigorous High Divide and make camp that night. She remembered that trip because she'd awakened in the middle of the night and found herself alone. She'd been frightened, assuming Rick had heard something, gone to investigate and was attacked by a wild animal.

As she paced the small area surrounding their tent, she called out his name four or five times. Then suddenly he appeared between the trees and apologized. He needed to relieve himself and didn't want to wake her. Although he acted like it was no big deal, he seemed hyper, agitated. When she asked him about it, he said he'd heard an animal stalking him on the fringes of the campsite.

They made sure the food bag was hanging high from a tree and went to sleep in the tent. It took a solid hour for her to drift off, hugging herself inside her sleeping bag. She'd wanted him to hold her that night for comfort, but he didn't touch her, and not just that night, but so many others. She began to think he no longer found her attractive, yet looking back she wondered if they'd drifted apart because he was ashamed of his criminal line of work.

Remembering that night got her thinking. What if his

stash was hidden in that area and he'd used their camping trip as an opportunity to hide the bearer bonds?

She stood and opened her door. "Quinn?"

No one answered. She wandered through the apartment and glanced out the sliding glass doors. She turned and noticed his bedroom door was ajar. Maybe he was resting. He must be sore from being hit by the car. She suddenly felt guilty for not staying out here and making him lunch.

As she approached the door, she heard the low timbre of his voice. "I don't need a lecture, Alex."

"I'm not lecturing, I'm offering another opinion."

"Which I didn't ask for."

"You can't keep all this guilt locked up inside, Quinn. Tell her and she'll understand."

"She'll understand that this was all my fault?"

"Don't be ridiculous," Alex said.

"Rick Bronson became a criminal because of me, he's dead because of me and now Billie's in danger, because of me. Everything bad that's happened to her is my fault."

Billie swung the door open. "Quinn Donovan, stop talking like that."

Quinn's blue eyes widened as if he'd been caught with his hand in the brownie bowl. Alex glanced at the floor and she could tell he was fighting a smile. He was glad she'd overheard their conversation.

"I'll give you two some privacy." Alex nodded at Billie and left the room, shutting the door with a click.

Quinn, who'd been standing behind his desk, collapsed in the office chair.

"What's with all the guilt?" Billie said.

He shook his head, but didn't answer. She went around to the other side of the desk. With a bent forefinger she tipped his head to look into his eyes. "None of this is your fault."

He stood and brushed past her. "Your husband lost his

job, his hope and his pride. He was forced to turn to crime to pay the bills."

"No one forced him—"

"I closed the plant." He spun around and pinned her with blazing blue eyes. "Did you know that? Me and two other silent partners shut it down because numbers were dropping. Just like that—" he snapped his fingers "—I shut the plant down and hundreds of people were out of work."

"As I recall you offered them severance packages and retraining."

"Meaningless." He paced to the window and crossed his arms over his chest. "You had a good marriage, a nice life and I'm responsible for destroying that."

Struck momentarily speechless, Billie wasn't sure how to pull Quinn out of this self-recrimination spin, but she knew one thing for sure: he'd done nothing wrong.

She thought about his stepmother's violent words. She'd convinced a little boy that he was responsible for his mother's death, that somehow he'd driven her into an early grave. Was he replaying that scenario in his head by convincing himself Rick's choices were a direct result of Quinn's business decisions?

"Quinn, look at me." She stepped close and waited. "Please?"

He slowly turned to meet her gaze, his eyes lit with guilt, anger and regret.

"Rick was a grown man. He made his own choices. No one pushed him into anything."

Quinn shook his head. She placed an open palm against his cheek.

He sighed. "Don't do that."

"Why not?"

"I don't deserve your compassion, not after what I've done."

"What, protected me? Gave me a home after Rick died and his family abandoned me?"

"Don't make me sound like a hero, Billie. I'm not a hero."

"In my eyes you are," she said with such admiration.

He studied her as if experiencing what she felt for him, for the first time.

She offered a tender smile and she thought he was going to kiss her—

Alex knocked on the door. "You both still alive in there?"

"Come on in," Quinn answered, not breaking eye contact with Billie.

"Sorry to interrupt, but I think one of the search-and-rescue victims is a girl who went missing early this morning from Waverly Harbor. I need to check it out."

"Are they okay?" Billie said. She'd completely forgotten about the text that was dispatched during church.

"No serious injuries. They've been transported to the hospital. Anyway, I didn't want to leave without saying goodbye. Billie," Alex said, giving her a brotherly hug. Then he turned to Quinn.

Billie noticed Quinn's slight wince in anticipation of the hug. He must still be hurting.

"I'll check in later." Alex gave Quinn a quick hug and smiled at Billie. "Take care of him for me."

"I'm trying," Billie said.

Alex left them alone and Billie turned her attention to Quinn. "All this time…" she hesitated "…you've been wallowing in blame?"

"I don't wallow, but the fact is, I *am* responsible." He wandered out of his room.

She followed him. "I knew you had an ego, but I didn't realize it was enormous."

"This has nothing to do with my ego." He went into the kitchen and opened the refrigerator.

"Sure it does. You made a smart business decision and that had to be the *only* reason my husband became a criminal. It couldn't be because of his weakness of character." She reached around him and snatched an apple out of the bowl on the top shelf of the fridge. "Quinn Donovan, a powerful man who changes lives with a stroke of his pen." She padded into the living room. He slammed the refrigerator door and followed.

"You had to sign paperwork to close the plant, right?" she continued. "To approve severance packages and retraining programs?"

He clenched his jaw, didn't answer.

"What's happening with the plant property?" she pressed.

"We've been trying to rezone it for retail."

"Which would keep tax dollars in Snoquamish County."

"That's the plan."

"Which will benefit everyone from the locals who want to shop and not have to drive an hour, to the high school kids who need after-school jobs to pay for college. It sounds wonderful, Quinn."

He shook his head and sat on the sofa. "You're talking me into circles."

"I'm speaking the truth." She sat next to him. "You took a bad situation and made it good."

"How can you say that?"

"Quinn, you're no more responsible for Rick's choices and my life, than you are for your mother's death."

He snapped his attention to her and Billie thought for a second she'd overstepped the boundary.

"It's amazing how well you know me," he said softly.

"Which I hope is a good thing?"

His cell phone beeped. "Donovan. Yes." He stood and paced to the sliding glass door. "You sure?…Okay, I'll swing by as soon as I can. Thanks." Quinn glanced at Billie. "I've gotta take care of something."

"What about dinner?"

"Go ahead and order room service. I'll eat when I get back."

"Are you sure you should be driving?" She stood and walked him to the door.

"No broken bones, no concussion. I'm fine, remember?"

"But you must be sore."

He smiled and fingered a tendril of hair behind her ear. "Don't worry about me. Relax, listen to music. But promise me you won't go anywhere."

"Promise."

"Thanks." He opened the door and greeted Phil, the security guard. "No one in or out."

"Yes, sir."

Quinn eyed Billie. "Don't look so worried."

"I can't help it. Trouble seems to be your shadow lately."

"I'll be fine." He walked away and glanced over his shoulder. "Shut the door, Billie."

She inched it shut. Placing an open palm against the inside of the door she whispered, "Be safe."

Quinn could have told Billie where he was headed, but then she would have demanded to go with him and he wouldn't risk exposing her to her husband's business associates.

Her husband's friend Stuart sounded concerned when he'd called about finding an old box of Rick's in his storage unit. Thinking it might help with the investigation, he contacted Quinn. Quinn didn't want to call Detective Issacs until he knew he was picking up more than a bunch of outdated paperwork.

He parked in front of Stuart's apartment building and noticed a soft glow reflecting through sheer curtains of the apartment window. With any luck Quinn would be back at the resort by dinner. The thought of sitting down for a quiet meal with Billie made him quicken his step. Their time together would end when they solved the burglary case, but until then he'd enjoy every meal, every moment with her.

It would have to last him a lifetime.

Once the thieves were caught and Billie was no longer in

danger, Quinn would do the right thing and say his good-byes. Yeah, and in the meantime he'd better stop kissing her.

Climbing to the second floor, he reflected on the almost kiss in his office earlier. It was everything he could do to stop himself from brushing his lips against hers, breathing in her floral scent and holding her until forever and then some.

"Can't happen," he muttered.

He approached Stuart's apartment and reached out to knock on the door. A crash echoed from inside.

"Stuart?" Quinn pounded on the door with his fist.

Silence.

Quinn pounded again. "Stuart, open the door!"

The door flew open and a man wearing a ski mask cat-apulted out of the apartment, shouldering Quinn against the wall. Stunned, Quinn stumbled and fell to the ground. Scrambling to his feet, he rushed into the apartment.

"Stuart?" He turned the corner into the living room and spotted him on the ground, blood staining his shirt.

Quinn dropped to his knees beside the body. Stuart's eyes fluttered open. "Opened the door. Thought it was you..."

Quinn called 9-1-1 and gave them the address. He grabbed a kitchen towel and shoved it against an apparent knife wound.

"The box," he wheezed. "He wanted the box."

"Where is it?"

"Trunk...of my car." He gripped Quinn's arm. "Billie..."

"What about her? Stuart, what about Billie?"

"They won't stop...until they get her." His eyes fluttered closed.

"Stuart, come on, buddy, open your eyes."

"Hands where I can see them!" a man shouted behind Quinn.

FOURTEEN

Four hours passed without a word from Quinn. Billie called his cell phone, but it went straight to voice mail. She was tempted to call Aiden, but she got the sense Quinn's business was off the resort property so Aiden wouldn't know about it.

She tried reading. What a joke. She'd land on a phrase like "moonlit lake" and her mind would drift to a memory of when she lived in Quinn's coach house. It was unusually warm one evening and she couldn't sleep, so she went out onto the back porch and enjoyed the cool breeze. A few minutes later Quinn wandered across his property to the dock and stood there, studying the calm lake.

And she'd watched him, wondering what was going on inside that head of his that made him take a midnight stroll. He'd fascinated her, this enigma of a man who paraded women in and out of his house, using them as some kind of emotional shield to keep Billie away.

It didn't take long for her to figure out there was more to Quinn Donovan than business deals and fleeting relationships. Much more.

She shook off the memory and called Quinn again. It went into voice mail. She left a message asking him to call her as soon as possible. By eleven she was frantic and called his brother, Alex. He didn't answer either.

After another twenty minutes of pacing, the phone rang.

"Hello?" she said.

"Billie, it's Alex."

"Thanks for calling me back," she said. "I'm worried about—"

"Quinn's fine. He's, uh, he's unable to talk, but I saw him a few minutes ago. He's okay."

"What do you mean unable to talk? He's not hurt is he?"

"No, no, nothing like that."

"Don't say it."

"What?"

"He's with a woman?"

"No," Alex said firmly. "It's not a woman and he's not hurt."

"Then where is he?"

A moment of silence, then, "He's in Lake Stevens lockup."

"What?"

"A man was murdered, Stuart Anderson."

"Stuart? Oh, no," she hushed, sadness coursing through her. "He was a friend of my husband's."

"Quinn was there when the cops arrived so they brought him in for questioning. Then they got a related call and are short staffed so they're letting him sit in lockup until they get back."

"Quinn did not kill anyone."

"You're preaching to the choir, Billie."

"You have to get him out."

"I'm working on it."

"Call Detective Issacs, he'll help."

"He hasn't returned my calls."

"I'm coming over."

"He'd want you to stay at the resort where you'll be safe. He didn't want me telling you what happened."

"When is he going to stop shielding me from everything?"

"My guess? Never."

"Tough. I'll bring my bodyguard. I'll see you in forty minutes." She ended the call and reflected for a moment, saying a prayer for Stuart.

Had Stuart's friendship with Rick caused his death? With

even more determination to put an end to this, she opened the door to Joe the security guard.

"Ma'am," he said.

"I need to get to the Lake Stevens Police Department. Immediately."

Forty minutes later Billie marched into the police station ready for battle. It was after midnight and she should be tired. Instead, she was energized by her determination to get Quinn out of jail.

Her conscience suggested that she was overstepping her bounds, that a restaurant hostess had no power to get a man out of jail. But she couldn't stand by and watch Quinn suffer because he'd involved himself in her life.

She knew she was in no position to negotiate Quinn's release, yet she had to see him, had to make sure he was okay.

She knocked on the door to the police department and someone buzzed her in. Joe followed her inside.

A uniformed cop greeted her. "Ma'am, is this an emergency?"

"I need to see Quinn Donovan."

"I'm sorry but—"

"I'm more sorry," she snapped. "It's my fault he's here."

"Why do you say that, ma'am?"

"He wouldn't have been at Stuart's apartment if he weren't looking into something regarding my husband's criminal activity. It's my fault and the least you can do is let me talk to him."

The officer sighed. "His brother is with him. This way."

She followed the officer into the cell area. Deep male voices drifted down the hallway.

"Enough already, Quinn," Alex said.

"I made a promise."

"To who? Billie?"

"No, to her husband."

Billie stopped short, stunned. The police officer hesitated beside her.

"Whoa, whoa. Rewind," Alex said. "Rick Bronson, the criminal?"

"Yes."

"You didn't even know him until the day you rescued them off the mountain."

"While we waited for the medics he begged me to look out for Billie. He said she deserved so much more than he was able to give her."

"But that's not why you're doing all this, is it?"

Silence.

"Quinn?"

"I made a promise, Alex. I intend to keep that promise."

The floor seemed to shift under Billie's feet. All this time Quinn had been offering her aid and assistance because Rick had asked him to? Quinn was keeping his word to a stranger, to a criminal?

No, it may have started that way, but Billie refused to believe he continued to help her—and kiss her—out of a sense of duty.

She took a deep breath and turned the corner into the cell area. Quinn spotted her and turned away. "What are you doing here, Billie?"

"I was worried about you."

"Alex told you I was fine. You put yourself in danger coming here."

"I'm in a police station with a police officer by my side and a bodyguard in the office, not to mention your brother, the cop. I'm perfectly safe."

"Maybe we should—" Alex motioned to the deputy and they left Quinn and Billie alone.

She leaned against the cement wall and studied him. He still wouldn't look at her.

"Why didn't you tell me you were going to Stuart's?" she asked.

"Because I knew you'd want to come with me and I didn't want to put you in danger."

"Right, because you'd made a promise to protect me."

He snapped his gaze to meet hers. "You heard that?"

"I did."

He paced his small cell. "That's probably a good thing. Now you know the truth."

"That my husband felt remorse? Yes, it's good to know he found his way back to grace in the end."

"No, I meant now you know my true motivation. I made a promise to a dying man to protect his wife."

"Which you've done brilliantly."

"Not sure I agree with that. Anyway, you can understand why I didn't want you to come with me tonight."

"No, I don't. We work much better as a team than we do apart. Haven't you figured that out yet?"

"Billie, you'd be standing right here beside me."

"There's no place I'd rather be."

Shaking his head, he paced to the opposite side of the cell. "I'm in jail."

"A misunderstanding. We'll clear it up shortly. Once we track down Detective Issacs, he'll make things right."

"Go back to the resort."

"As soon as you're released. We'll return together."

"I could be here all night."

Billie pulled a fiction novel out of her purse and sat down on the floor. "Works for me. I'm at the good part."

"What are you doing?" he said.

"Reading." She glanced at him. "What are you doing? Oh, right, feeling sorry for yourself." She waved him off, hoping her instincts were steering her in the right direction. "Let me know when you're done."

She focused on the pages, but sensed Quinn watching her

with an intense expression. The man had too much pent-up anger and resentment directed at himself. Until she convinced him to let it go, he'd be controlled by the unhealthy emotions like a marionette controlled by a puppeteer's strings.

Please, God, help me help Quinn.

The door clicked open and Alex stepped into the cell area. He glanced at Billie, then Quinn.

"I was worried because it got awfully quiet in here," Alex said.

Billie smiled. "We're fine. I'll stay and finish my book if that's all right with the officer."

"I'll check with him. You okay with that, little brother?"

"Like I have a say in anything that's happening around here," Quinn muttered.

Alex and Billie shared a conspiratorial smile.

The police officer came into the cell area and pulled out his keys. "My sergeant said to release your brother. We've got two witnesses at the apartment complex who saw a tall, husky guy wearing a ski mask fleeing the scene in a Ford Bronco."

"That's the guy who ran out of Stuart's apartment," Quinn said.

"Also, Detective Issacs called and confirmed that you're working with him." The officer unlocked the cell door. "Sorry for the inconvenience."

Quinn stepped out of the cell and extended his hand to Billie. "Unless you want to stay and finish your book."

"Wise guy." She grabbed his cool, firm hand and he pulled her to her feet. "Thanks."

A tender smile eased across his lips. "Let's go home."

Quinn didn't talk much during the car ride to the resort. They'd picked up his car at Stuart's apartment and she rode with Quinn, while Joe followed close behind.

When they got to the resort Quinn did a thorough search

of the apartment to make sure no one had been inside, then left to spend the night in a guest room.

Monday morning came and his mood improved a bit, but he still seemed withdrawn and pensive. He joined her for tea and fresh fruit at eight. He looked handsome in his navy suit and cream-colored shirt open at the neck. She wondered if he had business appointments today.

"Did you sleep okay?" she asked.

"Sure," he answered, not looking at her.

"Quinn, what's bothering you?"

He shot her a look.

"Other than the obvious," she added.

"Stuart found a box belonging to your husband, which is why he asked me to come by. Detective Issacs is bringing it over this morning for you to look through." He forked a strawberry but didn't eat it.

"And?"

He glanced up with tired, blue eyes. "Stuart said something before he…" His voice trailed off. "He said they wouldn't stop until they found you. It's like you have something or know something." He sighed. "I don't know anymore."

"Then I'll have to try harder to remember something that will help us."

"Those aren't good memories. I hate seeing you in emotional pain," he said.

She wanted to tell him if that were the case he'd stop pushing her away, but that was a conversation for another time.

"I appreciate that," she said.

He glanced at the phone on his belt and stood. "I'd better take this."

"As long as you don't ditch me again," she said.

With a slight smile, he wandered to the sliding door. "Cody, how's it going, buddy?" He went out onto the patio and shut the door.

She noted how tired Quinn looked, how beaten. It was almost as if he thought he'd already failed. But he hadn't. He'd kept Billie safe for the past week. Without him she'd be…

A shudder ran down her arms. She didn't want to think about what could have happened if Quinn hadn't made her welfare his priority. But was he motivated by his promise to Rick? Maybe at first, but something real had grown between them, and no matter how determined he was to fulfill his obligation and disappear from her life, she was just as determined to make him see it was okay to embrace their love.

"One thing at a time," she whispered to herself. First they'd solve the case and put Rick's disastrous decisions behind her. Then, somehow, she'd work on getting through to Quinn. She'd left him five months ago because she couldn't stand being pushed away when she knew, deep down, that he cared about her.

Someone knocked on the door. She went to answer and spotted Detective Issacs through the peephole. She opened the door.

"Good morning, Detective."

"Billie."

She motioned him into the living area. "Would you like some coffee or tea?"

"No thanks." He slid the box onto the dining room table and scanned the living room. "What, no Quinn?"

"He's on the patio taking a call."

"Good, I'm glad he's here."

"Why's that?" She started pulling items out of the box.

"Because I need to have a serious talk with that man."

"About?" She pulled out an old, empty, man's wallet.

"About me getting him out of lockup when I should have left him there for interfering with an ongoing investigation."

She snapped her attention to the detective. "He wasn't interfering. Stuart called him about the box."

"And Quinn should have called me, but he didn't. Maybe if he had we would have caught the guy."

"You can't blame Quinn for—"

"I gave him an order to call me if anything developed with the case and not go off half-cocked on his own. But he didn't listen, and now a man's dead."

"You can't blame Quinn for Stuart's death."

"Sure he can," Quinn said, stepping into the room.

She looked from Quinn to the detective, and back to Quinn.

"If you'd called me, I might have made it to the apartment that much sooner," Detective Issacs said. "Stuart might still be alive."

"You're right," Quinn said. "I should have notified you."

"I'm glad we agree. So, now you'll understand why I'm taking over protective custody of Billie and ordering you to distance yourself from this case."

"No, wait, don't I get a say here?" Billie argued.

Detective Issacs turned his attention to her. "Of course, but keep in mind, Quinn's inexperience has repeatedly put you in danger and his arrogance won't allow him to work with a team. Is this the kind of man you want to depend on for your life?"

"Yes," Billie said.

"You're not thinking rationally," the detective countered.

"Excuse me?" Billie said.

"Billie, he's right," Quinn said from across the room.

He was keeping his distance, which was worrying her even more.

"Quinn, if it weren't for you—"

"They might have solved the case by now. This whole thing has been mishandled on my part." He nodded at the detective. "I'll remove myself from the investigation. Billie's free to stay in my apartment. I'll be leaving town tomorrow."

FIFTEEN

Billie wanted to grab Quinn by the shoulders and shake some sense into him. Not a smart move considering the detective had accused her of being irrational. He'd probably call her downright crazy if she did that.

She knew what was happening. The detective, like Quinn's stepmother, had pressed Quinn's button, the one that made him feel worthless, like a failure.

Billie turned her attention away from the men and started going through Rick's items, trying to stay calm. Yet the thought of Quinn leaving increased her desire to solve this case, because only then could she challenge him about his feelings for her.

About the love she knew he felt as strongly as she.

She focused on the contents of the box, mostly paperwork, in the hopes of finding something critical to the case. After all, if Rick had hidden the box with Stuart, it must contain things he didn't want Billie knowing about. Out of the corner of her eye, she spotted Quinn cross the room.

"Quinn, I could use your help interpreting some of this paperwork," she said.

He froze midway through the living room and glanced at the detective.

"Go ahead," Issacs said. "Did you say you had coffee?"

"There's a pot on in the kitchen." Quinn sat down next to Billie.

She handed him a file folder and their hands touched.

Her breath caught at the expression on his face. She'd never seen anyone look so utterly lost.

"What am I looking for?" he said.

"You're asking me? I'm just the wife," she joked.

Quinn paged through legal documents. She leaned closer to read the paperwork. "What's that?"

"Apparently Rick bought a boat?"

"That's news to me."

She pulled out a manila envelope and sorted through old photographs of her and Rick, their first apartment, their five-year wedding anniversary. She shoved her melancholy aside and kept digging.

And that's when she found a strange key on an insurance company's keychain. "Okay, this is weird." She held it out to Quinn.

"What'd you find?" Detective Issacs said, coming into the room.

"A random key," Billie said.

"And apparently Rick Bronson owned a boat," Quinn offered. "Wonder if that's where he stashed the stolen property."

"Any idea where it's docked?" Issacs looked over Quinn's shoulder.

"Not yet."

Detective Issacs yanked his phone off his belt. "Great," he muttered as he took the call. "Issacs."

He motioned to Quinn and Billie that he was going into the hallway for privacy. The door slammed shut, leaving her and Quinn alone.

Not now, Billie, she reminded herself.

She redirected her attention to the pile of photos in front of her.

"That must be hard," Quinn said, nodding at the photographs.

"A little. But it's important to remember the good times,"

she said, flipping over a photo of Rick and Stuart standing in front of a cabin.

"Quinn, I recognize this photo from Stuart's place. Remember what Stuart said about them staying at a friend's cabin? What if it belonged to Rick?" She dangled the key between them. "What if this is the key to the cabin?"

"But how are we going to find it in thousands of acres of national forest?"

She nodded at the photograph. "I think I might know where this is. That's why it bothered me before." She pointed to the photo. "I recognized this vista from when Rick and I went camping once. I meant to tell you about it last night but got distracted. Rick disappeared on me in the middle of the night and returned all hyped up. It was weird."

The detective knocked on the door and Quinn let him in.

"I don't know how this happened, but my suspect made bail," Detective Issacs said.

"The bearded man?" Billie said.

"Yes, ma'am."

"But how—"

"Money, that's how," Issacs cut off Quinn.

"Well, I think we might have a lead." Billie showed the detective the photograph. "This same photo was at Stuart's place. I recognize this spot. Rick and I camped in that area and he mysteriously disappeared for a few hours one night. This could be where Rick was hiding the stolen goods."

"The bearer bonds," Issacs hushed. "I'll get a team assembled to investigate the cabin. Can you point it out on a map?"

Billie shook her head. "We didn't need a map. Rick knew where he was going."

"Do you think you can lead us there?"

"Wait a second," Quinn stood. "You're not seriously considering taking her out there. Talk about an easy target."

"We'll have plenty of manpower to protect her, don't you worry," Issacs said.

Billie could tell Quinn wasn't convinced.

"First things first. Let's find the boat," Issacs said. "If the bearer bonds are stashed there, we'll have no reason to find the cabin." He pulled out his phone. "Oh, and we won't be needing your private security anymore, Donovan. Our department can protect her just fine."

It was happening too fast. By one in the afternoon Issacs had assembled a small team to escort Billie into the mountains.

Quinn had hoped they'd find the bearer bonds on the boat, but no luck.

He stood outside the resort watching two cops and Issacs pack gear into the truck for the hike. Maybe Quinn was a screwup and kept putting Billie in danger, but he only felt confident that she was okay when he could actually see her.

When he was with her, looking into her big brown eyes.

"Don't look so worried," she said, approaching him. "I'll be with police officers."

"It's a habit I guess, worrying about you."

"Won't you be glad when that's over?" she teased.

But Quinn wasn't smiling. When this was over and he walked away—

"Ready?" Issacs called out to Billie.

Quinn placed his hands on her shoulders. "You've got your personal locator beacon, right?"

She slipped it out of her pocket. "Nothing's going to happen, Quinn. And once this is finally over, you and I need to have a talk, okay?"

He nodded.

"Let's go!" Issacs got into the front seat.

She leaned forward and kissed him on the cheek, quickly turned and went to the waiting truck. Quinn clenched his fist, feeling frustrated and utterly helpless. He wanted desperately to go along on this mission, and was peeved that Issacs didn't have more men accompanying them into the mountains. In Quinn's mind she could be hiking with a dozen law enforcement officers and it still wouldn't be enough.

Quinn wouldn't feel confident of Billie's safety until she was back home.

Home, as in Quinn's apartment. The place had only started feeling like a home since Billie moved in. Her essence, her positive energy and sense of humor filled his place with light and love.

And God. There, he'd admitted it: it was the first time he'd felt God's presence in his life.

The trucks pulled out and she waved from the backseat. He waved back, ignoring the pit growing in his stomach. Anxiety settled low, apprehension that he'd never see her again.

Aiden walked over to Quinn. "Hey, when you're done here I've got—"

"I'm done." Quinn ripped his gaze from the disappearing trucks and addressed his friend. "How can I help?"

"We're having some computer issues and the IT guy won't be in the area until tomorrow night. You want to give it a try?"

"Of course."

An hour later Quinn had identified the kink in the system and rebooted the computers. It had been time well spent, an hour of intense focus that distracted him from the tension twisting his gut into knots over Billie's safety. He had no reason to be anxious, he kept telling himself. Billie was in good hands.

He went to his place to make lunch. The moment he opened the door, he missed her. The apartment reeked of Billie from the neatly stacked magazines on his coffee table, to the teacup sitting on his kitchen counter. Even her floral scent lingered in her absence.

Man, he needed another project, another crisis to take his mind off Billie.

He opened the refrigerator and froze at the sight of a peanut butter and jelly sandwich covered in plastic wrap on the top shelf. A bright sticky note lay on top: *Enjoy with sliced apple. Love, Billie*

He shut the door. Love? Sure, why not. She was a thoughtful and compassionate woman who was motivated by love in most everything she did. He decided to save the sandwich for later and distract himself with work.

He checked email and made a few calls. It felt good to dive into work, even if his heart wasn't totally into it.

Twenty minutes later he lost focus, so he headed into the kitchen to savor the sandwich she'd made him. He grabbed it from the refrigerator and pulled off her note, placing it in his pocket with a smile. Leaning against the counter, he took a bite. It was the most delicious sandwich he'd ever tasted, and he'd eaten plenty as a kid. Without a loving mother around to care for him, Quinn had learned early on to care for himself, to make his own lunches and sign his own permission slips for school.

He smiled at the sandwich in his hand. It tasted so good because it was made with love, for him, by an amazing woman.

Someone knocked on the apartment door. Quinn put the sandwich down and went to open the door. Cody, with his right arm in a sling, stood in the doorway.

"Hey, man, it's great to see you," Quinn said.

"It's great to be seen."

"Come on in. I was eating lunch."

"Don't want to interrupt."

"You're not. It's just me and my PB and J. I'll make you

one if you're hungry, although it probably won't taste as good as Billie's."

"How's she doing, anyway?" Cody glanced into the living room.

"She's good. Not here."

"That's surprising. I didn't think you'd let her out of your sight until this case was done."

"It was about time the police stepped up to take the lead." Quinn grabbed his plate and headed to the dining table. They both sat down. "How's the shoulder?"

"Better. What's happening with the case?"

"Police think Rick Bronson's associates are trying to find bearer bonds he'd absconded with from a Vancouver burglary. They're trying to track down a cabin where Rick may have hidden the stuff he kept for himself."

"That guy was a piece of work. Stealing from thieves? That's asking for a world of trouble."

"Yeah, well, desperation will make a man do incredibly foolish things."

Cody glanced sideways at him. "We are talking about Rick Bronson, right?"

Quinn didn't answer.

"Quinn?"

"In my own desperation to protect Billie, I made some mistakes. The detective clearly pointed that out, so I agreed to remove myself from the case."

"Huh." Cody leaned back in his chair. "Who went on this trip to find the cabin?"

"Billie knew the location so Detective Issacs and his men took her up there."

"What men?"

"Issacs and two plainclothes officers picked her up about an hour ago."

"Quinn, the Echo Mountain PD has been down two men since April. I heard they can barely get their shifts covered so they're getting assistance from the Skagit County Sheriff's office."

Quinn slowly put down his sandwich. "Then the guys must have been with the county?"

Cody didn't look so sure. Fear clenched Quinn's gut.

"No, no, no," Quinn muttered, and began pacing his apartment. He whipped his phone off his belt and called Alex.

"Hey, little brother."

"How well do you know Detective Issacs?"

"Not well, why?"

"But you worked on a task force with him, right?"

"Yes, but it didn't last long and we didn't say more than a dozen words to each other. Why, what's going on?"

"He and two other men took Billie into the mountains to find Rick Bronson's stash, but my gut's telling me he might be involved in—"

"Careful there, buddy. This is a cop you're talking about."

"Forget it."

"Wait, give me a little time to look into Issacs before you do something drastic."

"I don't have time, Alex. He's got Billie." Quinn ended the call and rushed to the closet. He pulled out his pack and checked it for supplies.

"You have any idea where they went?" Cody asked.

"None."

"Quinn, there are thousands of acres of mountainous land out there. How are you going to pinpoint their location?"

"Their location, right. If I can get a hold of Bree's phone I can do a reverse signal trace."

Quinn called Bree, gave a condensed version of what was going on and asked her to stop by immediately with her phone.

In a matter of minutes Bree came by and Quinn got to

work locating the signal she'd received from Billie's personal locator beacon the other day.

"Come on, come on," he muttered, trying everything he could think of to track her signal. Bree and Cody hovered close by. Someone pounded on Quinn's door and Cody answered.

SAR team members Aiden, Harvey and Will marched into Quinn's dining room.

"What are you—"

"I texted them and told them what was going on," Bree interrupted Quinn. "I thought you'd need help once you pinpointed her location."

"What are you doing?" Harvey asked, looking over Quinn's shoulder.

"Reverse signal trace of Billie's locator beacon," Quinn said.

"Think it will work?" Will said.

Quinn didn't answer. If it didn't work…

Quinn's phone rang. It was Alex. He shoved it at Cody. "Can you talk to him?"

Cody spoke with Alex, while Quinn and the other men focused on Quinn's laptop.

"He's working on finding her location now," Cody said to Alex. "Yes…Uh-huh…I'll tell him. Thanks." Aiden walked back to the dining table. "He spoke with the Echo Mountain Police Chief. He's been keeping a file on Issacs due to questionable behavior like disappearing during a shift for hours at a time. Issacs told him he was heading into the mountains with two Skagit county deputies today."

Quinn glanced at Cody. "Call Alex back and see if he can find out if any Skagit officers were assigned to this case, or if Issacs is making it up."

"He wouldn't lie to his own chief, would he?" Aiden said.

"He would if he was never going back to work. Once he gets his hands on the bearer bonds he'll have enough money to disappear indefinitely." He glanced at the computer screen. "And Billie will be a liability."

The locator beacon lit up on the screen. "Got her."

"Are you sure the cop is a part of this?" Harvey asked.

"I won't take the chance." Quinn forwarded the beacon signal to his smartphone, stood and grabbed his pack. "If Issacs isn't involved and I find them, there's no harm, no foul. If he *is* involved…" Quinn shook his head and started for the door.

"Wait," Aiden said.

"No time, Aiden."

"We're coming with you."

Quinn turned to the team. Aiden, Harvey, Will and Bree nodded.

"If I'm right, this could be dangerous," Quinn warned.

"Which is why you're staying back," Aiden said to Bree.

"Hang on, Fiona and I could—"

"No, he's right, Bree," Quinn said. "Billie would never forgive me if anything happened to you."

Bree sighed. "Okay, but it's dangerous for you, too."

"We've got the climbing experience," Will said.

"And military experience," Aiden added. "Plus, they're amateurs."

"Greedy amateurs," Harvey added. "Greed makes people stupid."

Quinn kept hearing Issacs's snide comment about Quinn not being able to work with a team and how that had caused so many mistakes. It was a dig, another way to damage Quinn's self-confidence. As he considered the three men standing before him, he finally felt the strength of joining with others for a common goal: to save Billie.

"Meet me out front in ten," Quinn said.

Billie and the police officers hit the overlook in two hours. They probably would have made it sooner if Issacs's men were more experienced hikers. One of them had slipped crossing a stream and gotten soaked, and the other man struggled to keep up.

They got to a clearing and spotted a rustic cabin sitting on a patch of rugged property.

"That must be it," Issacs said.

They approached the cabin and she pulled out the key she'd found in Rick's box. A key someone had killed Stuart for?

She sighed. So much violence.

They approached the front door and she noticed the keypad lock. She pocketed the key. "Well, this is useless."

The detective peeked in the front window, but it was covered with something solid. "We've gotta get in there," he muttered.

"We could break the glass," one of the other officers said.

"Windows are covered from the inside. We need to go in through the front door." He glanced at Billie. "Any guesses at the code?"

"I have no idea."

One of the other cops narrowed his eyes in disbelief.

"Why would I lie about that?" she said, more than a little miffed.

Issacs kneeled and looked at the door. "Any special numbers in your family? Birthdays, anniversaries?"

"I could try a few things, I guess," Billie said.

Issacs moved out of the way and she tried a combination of her and Rick's birthdays, then their anniversary. Nothing.

"You should call a locksmith," she said.

"You probably know the code, Billie. Just think," Issacs pressed, his voice taking on an edge that made her uncomfortable.

She paced a few steps away from the door and remembered the last time she and Rick were together in the mountains, waiting for search and rescue to find them. She'd kept him alert by asking questions and engaging him in conversation. She knew he'd suffered a brain trauma, yet he still talked to her. At one point he'd begged her forgiveness for not being a better husband. She offered her forgiveness, even though at the time she didn't quite feel it in her heart.

With desperation in his eyes, he'd asked her to recall their first date in great detail, from the movie they'd seen to the flavor of ice cream they'd shared afterward.

He'd called it the best day of his life. At that moment, stranded in the mountains, their first date had been the most important thing on Rick's mind....

She spun around and went to the door. She keyed in the month and date of their first date: 0417. She heard a click and opened the door. The cabin was pitch-black and she hesitated before going in.

Detective Issacs drew his firearm and nudged her aside. He went in, the two cops close behind him. Her heart racing, she wondered if there were other members of Rick's team who knew about this place, and if they'd been here recently.

"It's safe," Issacs said from inside. "Come on in."

She stepped into the one-room cabin. One of the cops ripped a blanket off the window, shining light across two single beds and a desk. Detective Issacs analyzed a stack of boxes in the corner and nodded to the cops, who pulled them down and rifled through the contents.

Issacs pulled something out of a box and nodded at his men. "We can't risk them coming back for this. Keep watch and I'll take care of Mrs. Bronson."

SIXTEEN

Quinn, Aiden, Will and Harvey found the closest trail-head and made the climb. It wouldn't take long to catch up to Billie since Quinn and his men were practically jogging. Not unusual for SAR volunteers.

When a text alert went out, team members would often challenge each other to see who would get to the scene first to take the field command position. In this case it wasn't about taking charge as much as saving Billie's life.

Quinn's gut told him Issacs was dirty. He recalled the contentious interactions he'd had with Issacs and how the detective lied about being a close friend of Alex's. The red flags should have gone up sooner.

Harvey, who led the team, consulted a topographical map as he hiked the rugged trail.

Quinn looked at his phone for Billie's GPS signal. He'd downloaded the app for fun, never expecting he'd use it for a personal crisis.

"We're close," Quinn said.

Then his screen went blank. He swallowed and fought his rising panic. "I've lost reception."

"Lost it?" Will challenged.

"Reception is spotty out here, but we're right on top of her," Quinn said. "We'll use the natural cover to our advantage to neutralize Issacs's men. I'm sure they have firearms and since we don't, we need to be smarter than they are."

"Shouldn't be hard for a guy like you," Will snapped.

Will may not like Quinn, but Quinn knew how much Will cared about Billie. For that, Quinn would be eternally grateful and he'd find a way to get along with the guy.

Harvey turned a sharp corner and hesitated. Quinn and the other men stepped up to Harvey and eyed a cabin in the distance.

"That must be it," Quinn said. "They're probably inside. Aiden, see that rock face along the side of the property?"

"Yep."

"Can you and Will hike up to the top and set up make-shift anchors to rappel down the cliff toward the cabin?"

"Sure, what have you got in mind?"

"I'll distract them to draw them out."

"Actually I'll do the distracting." Harvey grinned and pulled out a handful of firecrackers.

"They'll hear the noise and come outside. I'll draw them close to the ledge then you and Will drop down on top of them. Four of us against three of them are pretty good odds." Quinn glanced at all three men. "Everyone good with that?"

They all agreed they were and spread out to take their positions. Adrenaline racing, Quinn rushed down a hill and zipped behind the house to position himself on the other side of it.

Then a horrible thought struck him: What if they'd already found the bearer bonds, killed Billie and left the scene?

No, he couldn't think that way. He had to stay hopeful. Suddenly he found himself needing to ask God for strength, no matter what the outcome.

Because Quinn didn't think he could survive losing the woman he loved.

A sudden chill of loneliness rushed through him. He needed Billie, needed her more than he'd needed anything in his life. She was the one person who believed in him, so much so she'd convinced Quinn he wasn't a bad guy, that his childhood antics hadn't driven his mother into an early grave.

"Please, God," he whispered. "I don't know how to do this but I've gotta try. Please, God, help Billie."

He waited below the cliff, his eyes trained on the house, but there were no signs of life.

"Check in," Quinn said into his radio.

"Aiden and Will in position," Aiden responded.

"Harvey is ready to make some noise," Harvey said.

"Let's do it," Quinn ordered.

A few seconds later the firecrackers popped and two men sprinted out of the cabin, guns drawn. Gripping his shoulder, Quinn stumbled and positioned himself just right. Issacs's men—a short bald guy and a tall blond one—jogged over to him.

"What happened to you?" the tall guy said.

"The bearded guy," Quinn gasped.

"You saw the bearded suspect?" the bald guy said.

"Yeah, he's close."

Without warning, the tall guy slugged Quinn in the gut and he fell to his knees.

"You're always messing things up, Donovan."

"Finish him," the bald guy ordered.

Aiden and Will dropped from above, colliding with the men before they could discharge their firearms.

The stunned gunmen struggled against their attackers. Aiden pinned the bald guy facedown and pulled his hands behind his back. Will wrestled with the other one, and Harvey rushed to help, but the man was doing a good job of fighting them off. Quinn was about to throw himself into the mix when the tall guy broke free and scrambled to his feet.

Will nailed him with a taser. The guy went down in a trembling heap. The two gunmen finally secure, Quinn, Aiden and Harvey eyed Will.

"A taser?" Harvey said. "Really?"

Will shrugged. "What can I say? I'm raising two girls."

Quinn eyed the cabin wondering why Issacs and Billie hadn't come out with them. Unless…

"You want company?" Aiden said.

"No, I got this." Quinn sprinted to the cabin and darted inside. No one was there. Not Billie, not Issacs.

Boxes of what Quinn suspected were stolen goods were piled from floor to ceiling against one wall.

Dread clawed its way through his chest. He spun around and went to the gunman.

"Billie?" Will said.

Quinn grabbed the bald gunman and flipped him over. "Where is she?" he ground out.

"Like I'm gonna tell you?"

Quinn lost it and slugged the guy in the jaw. Pain sliced through Quinn's hand. Aiden pulled him off the guy and got in his face. "Check the GPS signal."

Dazed with worry, Quinn pulled out his phone with a shaky hand.

Please, God...

Quinn eyed the screen. A signal popped up. "Got it."

"She'll be dead by the time you get to her," the bald man said.

Will kicked the guy in the ribs. Harvey yanked Will away from him. "Okay, man, we know," Harvey said, then looked at Quinn. "Aiden and I will stay back with these guys. You and Will go get Billie."

Quinn and Will took off in a full-blown sprint. Quinn pushed the crazy thoughts out of his mind, thoughts like he would be too late, never be able to hold her or kiss her again. They served no purpose and would only distract him from finding Billie, because he wasn't leaving this mountainous land without her.

Only, would he find her alive?

It was finally over. Billie and the detective followed the trail toward a rendezvous spot where another team would escort her to safety.

She sighed as she thought about what was waiting for her down below. Quinn. She'd told him that they needed to talk when she returned, and she'd meant it. It was time for both of them to come clean about their feelings for one another, and for Quinn to be honest with himself.

"What's the hurry?" Detective Issacs asked.

"I want to get home," she shot over her shoulder.

"You mean back to Quinn Donovan?"

"And my nice, peaceful life."

"Peaceful?"

She slowed down to allow him to keep pace with her. "I had finally found peace after Rick's death. It took a year, but I made it, and then that bearded guy showed up on the trail."

"Did I hear my name?"

Billie whipped around and found herself staring into the eyes of the bearded guy.

"What are you doing here?" Issacs said, grabbing Billie and pulling her behind him.

"I made bail. You knew that." The guy smiled.

"You shouldn't be here."

"Why not? You've got my bearer bonds."

"Everything's at the cabin," Issacs said.

She wondered why Issacs didn't pull out his gun and shoot the guy.

"Maybe." The bearded guy stalked toward them. "Maybe not. Either way, I can't depend on you to do your job."

The guy charged Issacs and they both went down. Billie took off in the opposite direction, racing uphill. Here she thought she was safe, that she could put this all behind her yet Rick's criminal boss had tracked her down. How was that possible?

She wanted to pull out her phone and call for help, but couldn't risk slowing herself down.

A shot rang out. She stumbled and kept running, tears forming in her eyes. She hadn't come this far to be killed by the bearded man. After all, he had no use for her now that they'd found the cabin with the bearer bonds and other stolen goods.

"Billie!" Detective Issacs called out.

She hesitated.

"Billie, it's okay!"

With a gasp, she stopped running and caught her breath. She leaned against a boulder and waited for Issacs to catch up to her. She surely didn't want to go down there and see a dead body.

"Rick, what did you get yourself into?" she whispered.

A few minutes later, Detective Issacs turned the corner. His jacket was ripped and there was blood on his arm.

"You're hurt?"

"I'm fine."

"You…is he…?"

"He's no longer a threat."

She sighed and closed her eyes for a brief second. It was finally over.

But when she opened her eyes, she didn't like the expression on the detective's face.

"What's wrong?"

"I'm sorry." He grabbed her arm and coaxed her backward.

"What are you doing?"

"Buying us some time."

"Us?"

"My men and I need a good twelve hours to disappear."

"Your men…you mean—"

"I truly am sorry your idiot husband involved you in this. You seem like a nice lady."

"Let me go!" she cried.

SEVENTEEN

Quinn felt Billie's cry resonate in his chest. As they sprinted uphill, he spotted Billie struggling against Detective Issacs. Issacs shoved Billie, but she grabbed on to a tree branch, fighting to keep from catapulting down a mountainside.

"Keep her safe," Quinn ordered Will.

Quinn rushed the detective as he gave her another shove.

"No!" Will shouted.

Issacs snapped his head around.

Quinn was only twenty feet away.

Issacs whipped out his gun.

Quinn dove…

And the detective's gun went off.

The bullet nailed Quinn in the arm but didn't stop his momentum. Quinn tackled Issacs, ignoring the burn of lead tearing through his flesh. They both went down. Quinn slammed Issacs's wrist against the ground to loosen his grip on the weapon. It finally sprang free of his hand.

Issacs slugged Quinn in the gunshot wound, spearing pain through his body. They rolled dangerously close to the steep drop, each scrambling for leverage.

Out of the corner of his eye, Quinn spotted Will grab Billie and pull her to safety.

"Quinn!" Billie cried. "Help Quinn!"

Quinn kicked his feet against the hard earth to maintain his position, but Issacs was on top, pushing Quinn even closer to the edge until his head was nearly dangling over the side. With all the strength he had left, Quinn slammed the heel of his palm against Issacs's chin and slugged him in the gut.

Issacs recoiled.

Quinn grabbed Issacs's jacket and flung him aside.

But instead of landing next to Quinn, Issacs rolled toward the drop.

Quinn scrambled to grab him.

But it was too late. Issacs plummeted down the side of the mountain.

Quinn collapsed and rolled onto his back, dreading what came next. He'd fought with and probably killed a cop. A dirty cop, but still a cop. Quinn would be in a mess of trouble when he made his way off this mountain.

"You okay?" Will asked.

Quinn eyed Will, holding Billie protectively against his chest.

"Yeah," Quinn said.

Billie started to push away from Will.

"Stay there," Quinn said. He didn't want her seeing his injury up close, or Issacs's body down below.

Will gently stroked her hair, encouraging her to stay put. She leaned into him, not taking her eyes off Quinn.

At that moment, Quinn realized how much Will loved her. Quinn knew the feeling.

Will was a good man with a promising future and two little girls. He could give Billie the stable life she deserved. What could Quinn give her? He didn't know how to have a healthy relationship with a woman. He'd screwed up so many in the past, including his marriage.

Quinn heard that Will had had a good marriage, a solid marriage. He knew how to make a woman happy.

And that's when Quinn knew what he had to do.

They hadn't spoken in private since Detective Issacs's accident on the mountain. Billie paced the waiting area in the hospital hoping to see Quinn, to make sure he was okay. The big talk would have to take place tomorrow or another day, once things settled down.

So much had happened in the past few days and it had happened so quickly.

"Hey, girlfriend," Bree said, walking up to Billie and giving her a hug. "How's he doing?"

"His brother and the police chief are with him. I think he's okay since he's up to talking."

"I'm so sorry this happened." Bree rubbed Billie's arm.

"Well, I'm relieved and thankful it's finally over."

"Giving you the opportunity to take care of other business?" Bree winked.

Billie smiled, appreciative of Bree's friendship.

"Billie?" Alex came out of Quinn's hospital room to speak with her.

"How is he?" Billie asked.

"Tired, but good."

"They aren't arresting him, are they?"

"No, there's enough evidence against Issacs and his men to clear Quinn of any wrongdoing. An SAR team recovered Issacs's body this morning."

"Was he…?"

"He didn't survive the fall."

"He got off easy," Bree muttered.

"What about the other men?" Billie questioned.

"They're trying to cut a deal in exchange for information."

"What kind of information?"

"Who was involved, a list of their jobs. Apparently after Rick died and you didn't turn anyone in, they assumed you didn't have anything on them."

"And they came after me now because…?"

"They'd waited ten months to cash in the bearer bonds, but they were missing from the Vancouver haul. They figured Rick stashed the bonds somewhere and you were their best shot at finding them."

"Then why try to run us down in the hospital parking garage?" Bree said.

"They weren't trying to run you down. Issacs ordered his men to kidnap you."

Billie shuddered.

"And if that didn't work…" Alex sighed and shook his head.

"They were going to kill me?" Billie said.

"They were going to find leverage," Alex said.

"You mean…?"

"Quinn. The bearded suspect wanted to use Quinn from the get go, kidnap him, threaten to kill him to convince you to cooperate, but Issacs said no."

"Because?"

"Quinn can be a handful. Issacs knew it. He thought the better strategy was to mess with Quinn's head by threatening you. Issacs knew that would throw Quinn off his game. Plus Issacs had your friend Will arrested to distract authorities from the real perpetrators, and throw you off, making you question those closest to you."

"My SAR friends," she whispered. "What about the jewels we found at my old house?"

"We're guessing those were Rick's first stash. He took them to see if anyone would notice. When they didn't, he moved on to to bigger items."

Billie sighed. "But it's finally over, right?"

"It is. You're safe."

"Can I see Quinn?"

"Sure."

Billie passed the police chief as she rushed to Quinn's room. She and Will had given their statements earlier and he'd gone home to check on his girls.

Billie stepped into the hospital room, steeling herself

against what she'd see: a bruised and beaten Quinn. Fortunately he didn't look too bad. She smiled. "Hey, you." She went to give him a hug, but hesitated because she didn't want to hurt him.

Quinn adjusted himself in bed. "I shouldn't even be in here. It was a flesh wound. I'm fine."

"They probably want to keep you overnight to keep an eye on your head injury."

"What head injury? What's my name again?"

"Very funny."

His smile faded. "Where's Will?"

"Home with his girls. What a crazy day, huh?"

"Yeah."

"Alex filled me in on everything."

"He's hovering. It's making me nuts," Quinn said.

"I'm so glad it's over and we can get on with our lives." She reached for his hand, but he pulled away.

"Quinn?" A sinking pit grew in her stomach.

"Will, he's a nice guy."

"So are you."

"Will really cares about you." Quinn glanced at her. "Maybe even loves you."

She wanted to say *so do you,* but those weren't her words to speak. Instead, she kept quiet and waited.

"The way he was holding you up there, protecting you," he continued.

"Quinn Donovan, are you jealous?" she teased.

But he wasn't smiling. She was losing him and she didn't know how to hold on.

"We said once this was over—"

"That we'd have a talk," she interrupted. "About us."

"There's nothing to talk about. I'll head back to Waverly Harbor and you'll stay here with your friends…" he hesitated "…and Will."

"Do I get a say in this?"

"We both do, but my side of this decision has been made. If you really think about it, you'll realize Will is the guy you should be with. He's the better man."

She clenched her jaw, wanting to give him a lecture he'd never forget. He adjusted himself and winced in such pain that she couldn't go on the attack, not tonight.

Instead of letting anger and frustration drive her actions, she opened her heart to compassion and love. She went to his bedside, stroked his hair and looked into his eyes. "I love you, Quinn. I will wait for you, as long as it takes, and you know I'm a very patient woman."

She kissed him on the forehead. "Be well."

She turned and left, fighting the tears welling in her eyes. It was the truth…only, would it be enough to make Quinn relinquish his shame and accept love?

Quinn got out of town as quickly as he could, staying away from the resort, from Billie.

Now, nearly a week later, he ached inside. Not from the bullet wound or the bruised ribs or any of his other bumps and bruises from his time protecting Billie. No, he ached for Billie.

Quinn spent most of the week at his lake house in Waverly Harbor, far enough away from Billie not to be tempted to swing by or even spy on her from afar. Somehow he thought if he were fifty miles away in another town it wouldn't be so bad.

He was wrong.

The intercom buzzed and his body ached as he got up to answer. Some days he felt like an old man he moved so slowly. But he'd heal eventually, at least physically.

He went to the intercom and pressed the button.

"Yeah?"

"It's your brother. Let me in."

Quinn sighed and pressed the button to open the gate. He wandered to the front door. As the car pulled up the drive,

Quinn noticed Alex had a passenger. Billie? His heart leaped with hope. Then he started to panic. He hadn't shaved this morning nor had he combed his hair. He wasn't planning on seeing anyone.

As the car edged closer, he realized it wasn't Billie. It was her friend Bree.

He wandered out onto the porch and sat in an Adirondack chair.

Alex parked and Bree got out carrying a foil-covered plate in her hands. She headed to the porch and Alex followed.

"I found her asking for directions to the lake house so I figured I'd give her a ride," Alex said.

"How gentlemanly of you," Quinn said.

"That's what they tell me."

"Billie got Grace's recipe for monster cookies and made you a few dozen." Bree sat in a chair and slid the plate on a table between them. "She would have come herself, but…" Bree glanced down.

"What?" Quinn sat straight. "What's wrong, is she okay?"

She cast a quick glance at Alex.

"What's going on?" Quinn pressed.

"She's not okay, Quinn." Bree looked him firmly in the eye. "She's suffering from a broken heart because the man she loves is a coward. There, I said it. I promised her if I ever saw you I wouldn't speak my mind. Heck, she doesn't even know I'm here."

"Wait, but you brought cookies she made for me."

"She made them for you in the hopes you'd return to Echo Mountain, but I think it made her feel closer to you to have your favorite cookies around. That's all she's been doing—working and baking, oh and going to church. She stops by every day to say a prayer for you, not that you'll come back, but that you'll find peace. It makes me crazy."

Bree stood. "Here you're making her life miserable and all she wants is for you to be at peace and happy."

"But Will Rankin—"

"She doesn't love Will Rankin!" Bree planted her hands on her hips and shook her head. "I promised myself I wouldn't lose it, but someone had to do something. She thinks you love her, and I don't have the heart to tell her she's wrong, but I know she's wrong because if you loved her you'd be with her right now instead of hiding out, fifty miles away. If you do love her but you're staying away, then you're a fool because that kind of love is a gift from God. We all don't get to experience a love like that." Her voice cracked. She cleared her throat. "If you don't love her, fine. But please tell her so she can get on with her life." She stormed off the porch.

"I'll be right there," Alex said, then eyed Quinn.

"What?" Quinn challenged.

Alex thought for a second. "What she said." He turned and marched off the porch.

Quinn watched them drive off, processing Bree's outburst. She drove all this way to scold him? It shouldn't surprise him—she was Billie's best friend and when you were friends with Billie you developed a visceral need to protect her.

Leaning back in the chair, he eyed the foil-covered plate. She'd been baking in the hopes he'd come back. She wanted him back.

It sounded as if she'd been in as much pain as he had this past week. He peeled off the foil and found a hand-written note addressed to Quinn:

With all my love, forever and always, Billie.
Corinthians 13:4–8

It had been a week of recovery and grounding. Billie took a few shifts at the restaurant but wasn't up to working a full-time schedule yet. She was taking it easy, trying to nurture herself.

It all seemed like a dream, not all bad, yet painful once she awakened. Quinn was gone, out of her life, and she felt even emptier than before when she'd left his guesthouse in Waverly Harbor.

Because this time she'd felt an intense love develop between them, and it wasn't one-sided. She knew he cared deeply for her.

Yet words would not open his heart to what he was relinquishing. She guessed he was sacrificing himself so she could be with Will. That would be fine if she loved Will, but she didn't. He was a nice man and a good father. But Billie's heart belonged to Quinn and she wouldn't allow Will to marry for anything less than complete and true love. She hoped he understood. He said he did, although he'd looked hurt after she'd spoken with him a few days ago.

She added him to her daily prayer list, hoping he'd meet a wonderful, caring and nurturing woman to be his life partner.

A bell dinged indicating a text message. Her breath caught. Could it be Quinn?

"Silly," she muttered, grabbing her shoulder bag. It was probably Bree letting her know she was waiting downstairs to give Billie a ride to church. She glanced at her phone. Sure enough, it was Bree.

Yet every time the phone dinged with a text or call, a part of her thought it was Quinn wanting to make things right. Bree tried to get Billie to take the offensive and go after Quinn, but Billie felt he needed to come to the realization on his own that he was, in fact, worthy of her love and that love could heal his scars from the guilt and resentment he carried around on a daily basis.

She locked her apartment and went downstairs to Bree's

car. It was a beautiful, sunny day and Billie's spirits suddenly lifted.

"Hey, Bree," she said, getting into the car.

"Good morning, girlfriend."

They took off for church, Bree chatting away about a group of new guests at the resort and the K9 SAR meeting later that afternoon. When she didn't mention Quinn, Billie was both relieved and a bit sad.

"You okay?" Bree questioned.

"Yeah, fine. I'm kinda surprised you didn't start in on me about Quinn again."

Bree cracked a crooked smile. "I've got bigger issues than your love life, Wilhelma."

"What did you call me?"

Bree chuckled.

"What issues?" Billie pressed.

"Today is the qualifying test for K9 candidates, and I've got something special planned."

"Bree, they're dogs. Go easy on them."

"They have to be smart dogs so they can find injured hikers in the mountains. Whichever ones are able to find me today will be the best of the pack."

"When are you going out?"

"About two. Wanna come? You can hide with me."

"No, thanks."

"Okay, but Mom's having a family dinner later if you want to stop by."

"I'll think about it."

"Don't think—just come."

Bree pulled into the Echo Mountain Church lot and parked.

"I'm surprised you didn't pick up your mom for church," Billie said.

"She's getting a ride with Uncle Chuck."

They got out of the car and headed for church.

"You mean the family friend who's also the police chief of Marion Falls?" Billie said.

"That's the one. I thought they should have private time."

"Well aren't you the little matchmaker?" Billie teased.

"You have no idea. I'm working on Aiden next."

"Good luck with that. He seems pretty focused on work and on search and rescue."

"Ah, but a life without love is a life half lived, don't you think?"

Suddenly a man stepped into their path, a tall, handsome man with striking blue eyes. He looked like Quinn, wait… it *was* Quinn. Billie stopped short.

"Breathe, girlfriend," Bree said.

Quinn approached them wearing a nervous smile. Billie knew it was the nervous one because she knew all of his expressions and most of his moods.

"Bree," he greeted.

She smiled. "Quinn. You've come an awfully long way for church."

"How true," he said, gazing into Billie's eyes.

"I'll save us a few seats." With a knowing smile, Bree left them alone.

Quinn reached out and Billie slipped her hand in his.

"'Love is patient, love is kind.'" He smiled. "I looked it up."

"You're here," she hushed.

"You made me cookies."

"I know, but—"

"You know the part that really got to me?"

She shook her head, still stunned that Quinn was standing here holding her hand.

"'It always protects, always trusts, always hopes, always perseveres,'" he said. "Just like you. You're a kind of love I've never experienced, Billie. Please forgive me for not recognizing it sooner, for being…" he hesitated and glanced at their hands "…for being scared, I guess."

"Oh, Quinn, you have my forgiveness and my love." She threw her arms around his neck and clung tight, letting the tears of joy trickle down her cheeks. He stroked her back in such a calming, tender way.

She broke the embrace and he frowned with worry. "You're crying."

"I'm happy, Quinn, so incredibly happy."

"You haven't heard the best part." He dropped to one knee and pulled a black box out of his pocket. "Will you marry me?"

She slapped her hand over her open mouth, so humbled and overjoyed.

"Is that a yes?"

She nodded enthusiastically, unable to speak.

He took the ring out of the box, slipped it onto her finger and stood. It was a beautiful, solitaire diamond in a white-gold setting. Quinn's proposal was everything she'd ever dreamed of.

No, it was better.

With that playful smile of his, he framed her cheek in his hand, leaned forward and kissed her. He tasted perfect, of love and hope; of infinite possibilities between a husband and wife.

The ringing of church bells sounded behind them. He broke the kiss and smiled. "Shall we?"

"Are you…sure?" she said.

"With all my heart."

Interlacing his fingers with hers, Quinn led Billie toward the house of God and a wonderful life together.

* * * * *

Look for more books in Hope White's
ECHO MOUNTAIN *miniseries later this year.*
You'll find them wherever
Love Inspired Suspense books are sold!

Dear Reader,

It's with great pleasure that I present Quinn Donovan and Billie Bronson's book. Many of you met them in *Safe Harbor* and have written to me asking when you could read Quinn's story.

Quinn had the same effect on me when I wrote Alex's book. As a matter of fact, Quinn was so charismatic, I had a hard time keeping him from elbowing his way onto every page of *Safe Harbor.*

Quinn's journey has been a rough one, losing his mother when he was young and being convinced that her death was his fault. But luckily Quinn is surrounded by people who love him and exemplify how the love of God can heal one's soul.

We're taught a lot of things during our childhood that follow us throughout our lives. If Quinn Donovan has taught me anything it's that sometimes we need to do a little personal reflection, perhaps through prayer, to determine if those long-standing beliefs we've been carrying around help us or work against us as we take our personal journeys toward grace.

Wishing you peace and inspiration,
Hope White

Questions for Discussion

1. Did you understand Billie's need to hike alone into the mountains for closure? Have you ever needed closure and if so, how did you find it?

2. Could you appreciate Billie's need to keep Quinn at an emotional distance?

3. Did you consider Billie's relocation to Waverly Harbor and then to Echo Mountain as running away, or finding her way through tumultuous times?

4. It was pretty obvious Quinn cared about Billie from the beginning of the story. What do you think stopped him from pursuing a relationship with her?

5. What do you think inspired Quinn to be a part of the search-and-rescue team?

6. Did you admire Billie for being able to see through Quinn's facade, or did you think her unwise?

7. Have you known people who presented themselves one way, but who you suspected were something else? How did you best communicate with them?

8. Did you think Billie encouraged Quinn in a nonthreatening way to find God, or was she too enthusiastic?

9. Did you get the impression Quinn was ready to accept God into his life? If so, what were the signs?

10. What did you think about Billie's feelings for Will Rankin? Did you think she should have considered him as a boyfriend instead of Quinn?

11. Did you think Billie developed strength throughout the course of the book? If so, what examples can you share?

12. Did you sense something was off when Billie went into the mountains to search for the cabin at the end of the book? If so, what piqued your concern?